THE
CURIOUS
~TALE OF THE~
LADY
CARABOO

ALSO BY CATHERINE JOHNSON:

A Nest of Vipers
Brave New Girl
Sawbones

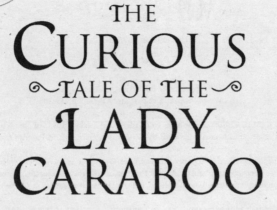

THE
CURIOUS
TALE OF THE
LADY
CARABOO

CATHERINE JOHNSON

CORGI BOOKS

THE CURIOUS TALE OF THE LADY CARABOO
A CORGI BOOK 978 0 552 55763 4

Published in Great Britain by Corgi Books,
an imprint of Random House Children's Publishers UK
A Penguin Random House Company

Penguin
Random House
UK

This edition published 2015

1 3 5 7 9 10 8 6 4 2

Copyright © Catherine Johnson, 2015
Cover photograph copyright © Bella Kotak, 2015

Penguin Random House is committed to a sustainable future for our business, our readers
and our planet. This book is made from Forest Stewardship Council® certified paper.

MIX
Paper from
responsible sources
FSC
www.fsc.org   FSC® C018179

Set in Sabon 11/16pt by Falcon Oast Graphic Art Ltd.

Corgi Books are published by Random House Children's Publishers UK,
61–63 Uxbridge Road, London W5 5SA

www.randomhousechildrens.co.uk
www.totallyrandombooks.co.uk
www.randomhouse.co.uk

Addresses for companies within The Random House Group Limited
can be found at: www.randomhouse.co.uk/offices.htm

THE RANDOM HOUSE GROUP Limited Reg. No. 954009

A CIP catalogue record for this book is available from the British Library.

Printed and bound in Great Britain by CPI Group (UK) Ltd, Croydon, CR0 4YY

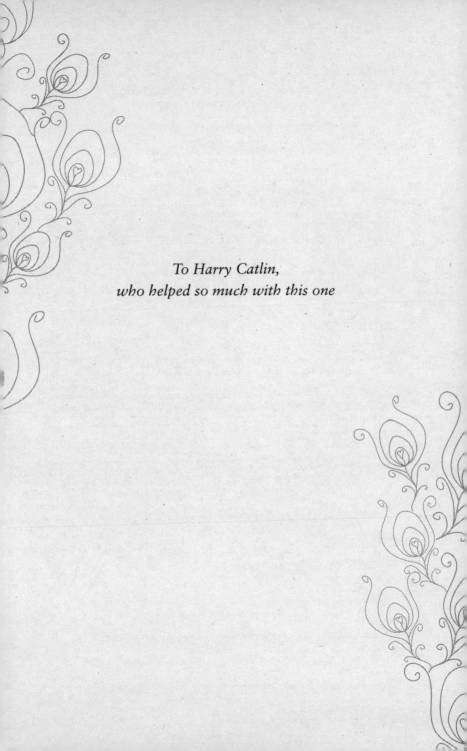

To Harry Catlin,
who helped so much with this one

CONTENTS

FROM THE BATH HERALD

Oh! aid me, ye spirits of wonder! who soar
In realms of Romance where none ventur'd before;
Ye Fairies! Who govern the fancies of men,
And sit on the point of Monk Lewis's pen;
Ye mysterious Elves! Who for ever remain
With Lusus Naturaes, and Ghosts of Cock-lane;
Who ride upon broom-sticks, intent to deceive
All those who appear pre-disposed to believe,
And softly repeat from your home in the spheres
Incredible stories to credulous ears;
With everything marvellous, everything new,
We'll trace a description of Miss CARABOO . . .

And where did she come from? and who can she be?
Did she fall from the sky? did she rise from the sea?
A seraph of day, or a shadow of night?
Did she spring upon earth in a stream of gas-light?
Did she ride on the back of a fish or sea-dog?
A spirit of health, or a devil incog.?

THE END OF MARY WILLCOX

On the Bristol road,
just outside Malmesbury
4 April 1819

They hit her from behind.

It didn't take much to fell the girl, on account of the
fact that she had been walking for the past seven days
and eaten very little, so was close to utter exhaustion.
She did not think, in the state she was in – caked with
dirt from hard travelling – that any man would look
twice upon her. Not in *that* way. She knew what to do,
what to say when men looked longer than was decent.
But she had felt powerless and weak since she had lost
the baby. Like an empty ghost.

She had heard of this happening to girls, both in
Devon and in London, acting the coquette and suffering the consequences. But she had done nothing,

not a word, not a smile; she had kept her head down, afraid that she looked like a savage, her hair full of twigs from sleeping in hedges and barns, her slippers worn quite through. She had done nothing.

The men were laughing. One pushed down hard, a booted foot in the small of her back. The girl hadn't the strength to struggle, nor even the breath to cry out.

There were two of them, and she could not bear to open her eyes to look, even though she could smell the cider on them, and feel their breath on her neck as they pulled and tore at her clothes.

'Ent never seen an arse as brown as this!'

'It's flatter'n a boy's! Jesus's bones! You sure she's a maid?'

'How would you know a maid's arse, eh? I heard it's only chickens have made your acquaintance!' The laugh came out as a snort.

'Chickens and your ma!'

They both laughed this time, and for a few moments the girl thought that perhaps they were both so taken with their own wit, they would forget she was there. She concentrated all her strength and tried to inch herself along the ground.

The laughing stopped.

''Ere, is our maid wriggling herself away?'

Her arms were dragged back behind her and her face pushed into the dirt.

The girl murmured a prayer, but she knew that the Lord did not look kindly on girls such as herself. If he did, she would have had the means to pay for a coach some of the way from London to Exeter, perhaps even the whole fare, maybe somewhere to sleep that had a roof. As it was she had prayed hard every night, and never so much as a penny found its way into her purse. She had only herself to rely on, to believe in – hadn't her short life proved this? Other people, men especially, bought only pain and suffering. Here, she thought, face down in the leaf mould, was more proof. Perhaps God thought she deserved no more than this.

So if praying would have no outcome, maybe she would be better off wishing. She would wish for wings so she could leave her attackers confounded on the ground and fly, up and away, and all the way home. She would shake her wings free of her short travelling jacket, the one the Magdalenes had given her, and the men would stand back open-mouthed as she rose up into the air. If she had wings, the girl thought, she could travel around the country fairs and fill her cap with coins till it overflowed. She wished hard.

'Hold her, boy!'

The girl did not need holding, she was so tired. She

was lying under the trees face down in the dead leaves, where the cherry blossom drifted down like pink snow and the afternoon light dappled green and gold through the branches. It should be beautiful. She could feel the air on her nakedness and it was cold.

There was the sound of belts unbuckling.

The girl knew it should not matter because she was ruined already. She felt the tears running down her face and could not wipe them away as her arms were pinned behind her.

If only she had been born in another time, in another place, as another girl. Not a cobbler's daughter from Devon, nor even a girl with wings, but maybe an Amazon warrior woman who could turn on her attackers. Better still, a fighting princess, a beautiful girl with a dagger at her waist and a quiver of magical arrows. They would not dare touch her then.

When the pain became worse, she thought of little Solomon, the one good thing that had come from her existence. He had never breathed the air, though he had come into this world a month ago this day, grey and still.

Perhaps, if she would not live long enough to make her peace with her father, this was her time.

The girl screwed up her eyes tighter and tried to shut out where she was and what was happening behind her.

She pictured Solomon, his tiny body swaddled and still, perfectly beautiful in death.

Perhaps these farm boys – the girl thought they smelled like farm boys – would do her the service of dispatching her quickly. She did not imagine that St Peter would stand aside and admit her to Heaven, after all that had happened to her.

But surely Hell could not be any worse than this.

1

THE GIRL FROM NOWHERE

Knole Park House
Almondsbury
Near Bristol
April 1819

Cassandra Worrall was bored. She felt utterly and completely trapped; immobile and immoveable – like the ship in that terrifying book her brother Fred had left with her when he went back up to school after Christmas. *Frankenstein*, it was called, and although entirely different to the usual gothic romances Cassandra favoured, it had been utterly thrilling. And it began with a ship held fast in a desert of ice.

Cassandra was not trapped in ice, but suffocated by fields of nothingness, by acres and acres of boredom made real as good English earth. Outside the window, the velvet-green park stretched away to the trees. Beyond the trees, a full half-mile off, lay the village, the church spire just visible. She sighed.

'Cassandra! *Attention s'il-vous-plaît!*' Miss Marchbanks looked sour. She always looked sour. When Cassandra asked her parents for French lessons she had imagined speaking the language of romance, not long hours in the airless schoolroom copying lists of verbs. Worse still, instead of employing a native speaker, as her friend Diana Edgecombe's family had, her parents had engaged their old governess, Miss Marchbanks, a woman who could render any fascinating thing as dull and brown as ditchwater.

Inside the schoolroom the air was warm and still; the only sound was the ticking of the large clock cutting the silence into bars. Downstairs, she knew her mother was busy with her ladies' circle – Cassandra had been happy to avoid it, but now she thought she would rather sit through one of her mother's anthropological discourses on the habits of the Pequot or the Nipmuc or the Mohican, or whatever group of happy carefree woodland peoples were to be discussed this month, than endure another hour of French with Miss Marchbanks. At least, she thought, she had not been obliged to take tea with the imperious Lady Gresham, who had arrived that morning. If only she had brought her son with her . . . But soon, Cassandra thought, Edmund Gresham, along with her brother, would be home from school, and then no doubt he would visit.

Edmund. She let her thoughts turn to him as Miss Marchbanks droned on. He was her brother Fred's oldest school friend and quite the handsomest man she had ever met. And it was not just his figure and face, which were straight out of the latest romance – his manner, too, was so modern, so daring. During the reel at the New Year's Ball he had held her so tightly that even thinking about it now, all these months later, caused her to catch her breath. He had not written to her since then, but Lady Gresham had assured her he barely wrote to anyone, and that he was always enquiring after Knole Park . . . He must, after all, be quite busy, preparing for his tour of Europe. He would not be bored. Not as she was now.

'Miss Marchbanks,' Cassandra said. 'Since it is three o'clock, and the weather is good, may I go out now, please?' Miss Marchbanks did not look up from the page, although one eyebrow was raised. Cassandra went on, 'Zephyr is in need of some exercise.'

'Well, Cassandra, let me see.' Miss Marchbanks held out her hand. 'If your work is correct . . .'

Cassandra passed over her copy book. 'I had not thought that French would be so tiresome.'

'Miss Cassandra, I do believe the French lessons were at your own request?'

She said nothing. She had imagined romance and travel and the possibility of Alps, lakes, glaciers. Not verbs.

'French is a very desirable accomplishment for a young lady,' Miss Marchbanks said.

Cassandra pushed herself up from her desk. 'Fred learns science at school. He said that last term they had a man come in to demonstrate electricity. He said you could see it jump across the air, glowing orange like a kind of lightning. Imagine! Just like Professor Frankenstein's experiments!'

Miss Marchbanks harrumphed. 'A most sensational and overstimulating novel. I am not sure that novels do the brain any good – all those ideas heat the blood, don't you know?' She paused, shaking her head. 'You need to learn to apply yourself, Cassandra Worrall. I have never known a girl so fickle and eager to jump from one thing to another. When you began your studies you were so keen. Your brain is young and unformed, a weather vane changing direction every few moments. I am sure you will find the French language a useful accomplishment when you are grown up.'

Cassandra seethed, but bit her tongue. Poor Miss Marchbanks had probably never been admired. Cassandra knew she was quite grown up enough. The Ball at the Edgecombes' had been a success – she had surely turned heads, even if the none of the young men in attendance had been half as handsome or a fraction as interesting as Edmund Gresham.

'Cassandra,' Miss Marchbanks told her, 'you may take your leave. But if you intend to go out, make sure that silly grin is off your face or you will surely be mistaken for an idiot.'

Cassandra was out of the schoolroom and across the landing before the governess had finished her sentence. She lifted up her skirts and took the steps at a run; past the painting of her mother's family in Philadelphia in America, past the marble bust of her father that the bank had given him, past the dainty Chinese drawing room, Mama's pride and joy, pale pink and blue in the not-quite-latest fashion, past the library where Father's books on finance and Mama's books on all the countries of the world lined the walls – then across the black and white marble-tiled hall and out into the sun.

Cassandra turned Zephyr up the hill, urged him on into a canter and let her mind wander.

Every night she thought about Edmund, imagining all sorts of contrivances whereby Fred invited her and Mama to London – no, not Mama, just her; they would travel together and she would stay at the house of some aunt, or perhaps a relation from America who was just off the boat. This imagined aunt would have a house in one of the smarter new streets in St James's, and would be younger than Mama. Fred and Edmund would call round and take her out for a walk, and she would be wearing . . . This part of the reverie was always the most difficult. Her cream muslin with a new sash, cornflower blue to match her eyes? Or the new Indian print with the neckline Mama thought too daring? Or better still, a dress entirely of her own devising, in lilac with some satin trim. Oh, and she would have some new slippers too . . .

Once she had decided on her gown and her hair, there was merely the matter of getting Fred out of the picture. She had imagined several scenarios in which Fred had to assist a passer-by whose horse had cast a shoe, or perhaps a stray dog needed to be caught – in any case, exit Fred, and there she was, alone with Edmund, in the best possible gown, in London.

He would look at her the way he had done at the ball – his eyes intense, almost desperate. And she would feel that power over a man experienced by the heroines she read about. She thought of him kissing her, his lips on hers, his body pressing into hers, and she was so involved she did not realize that her eyes were shut and Zephyr was about to jump a hurdle gate that lay across the track to the village.

'Oh!' The landing unseated her for a moment and Cassandra clung on for dear life, while Zephyr, true to his name, galloped like the wind down towards the village. She sat back and pulled hard on the reins, hoping to slow him down. Zephyr tossed his head – he was cantering now, slowing a little. Just when Cassandra thought she had him under control, he stumbled, and the reins were tugged out of her hand. Then Zephyr knew he had his head, and he tossed his mane and was off again at full pelt. Unable to reach the reins, Cassandra bent low, took a handful of mane in her hand and threw her other arm around his neck. She resisted the urge to scream or yell – she was after all a more than competent rider – and said to him, 'There, there, Zeph!' in what she hoped was a calming way.

Zephyr had flattened out into a long thin streak of iron grey, and Cassandra, seeing the track hurtle past under his feet, imagined that perhaps this near-death experience – maybe a broken ankle or wrist, nothing serious or scarring – might necessitate Fred coming home early from school, and Edmund too. Then the thought of some real harm – a blow to the head rendering her insensible, a cut to the face which might spoil her features – sent her giddy with fear. Mud flew up and spattered all over her as the horse careered towards the village.

'Zephy! Stop!' Cassandra knew she sounded pathetic, and naturally Zephyr took no notice. She realized it was merely a matter of time before she fell off. She closed her eyes and gritted her teeth. At least she would die knowing that a young man had held her; had held her so—

Zephyr's hooves clattered and splashed to a halt. Cassandra opened her eyes. This was not heaven. This was the village pond. Thank goodness she was still in her seat. She sat up. Then Zephyr gave a snort and shivered, making every bone and hair on his body twitch and ripple, and Cassandra, having stayed on while he flew down the muddy track, fell off into the filthy water, surrounded by a knot of small children laughing louder than thunder.

She got up. 'Stop it!' she yelled at them. 'Stop it at once!' She recognized the taller of the children. 'Robert Shaston, and you, Jonathan, the smith's boy! I will tell my—' She was about to add 'father' when her foot slipped on something indescribably slimy and she fell down again.

The laughter grew even louder. The whole village would be here soon. Zephyr had his head lowered to drink, swishing his tail at the flies, only pausing to give a little snort every so often, as if joining in with the village rabble.

Cassandra picked up the reins. She was aware that she was drenched from head to foot and splattered with mud, she felt she might burst into tears at any second. She knew she must get back on the horse and ride home. Her riding coat, pale blue and of the finest wool, was filthy. However would Mrs Bridgenorth restore it? She would hurry home as fast as she could, slip into the house through the stables, and hope to God, and all that was fair and just, that Mama's ladies would be so taken up with engravings of semi-naked American Indians that they wouldn't notice.

'Get off with you!' she shouted at the children, but they stood their ground, pointing and laughing.

'Come on, you lot, ent you got something to do? Here, miss, let me take the horse.'

The children scattered. She looked up. A young man with thick dark hair was shooing the children away.

'Are you all right, Miss Worrall?'

Cassandra stared at him but couldn't place him. She knew every soul in the village. Her parents were the residents of Knole Park, the biggest and most important house in the district. But this young man, wading towards her through the pond, was a stranger, she was sure of it.

'Will – William Jenkins from the Golden Bowl.' He ran his hand along Zephyr's neck and the horse greeted him like an old friend. 'You don't remember me, do you, Miss Worrall?'

'Of course I do,' Cassandra lied. She swept the wet hair away from her face and realized, too late, that she had merely transferred the black mud of the village pond from her hand to her cheek.

She waded out of the pond, attempting to pull Zephyr along behind her. Zephyr didn't move.

William Jenkins gave the horse a firm thwack across his hind quarters and he obediently stepped out after her.

'I could have managed!' Cassandra snapped.

'I am sure of it, miss.' Will was looking straight at her with his cool blue eyes, as if he were her equal.

'Thank you. I will go home now.'

'If you'd like, miss,' he said, 'you could clean yourself up at the Bowl – well, not in the inn, naturally, but I could let you in the kitchen. There's no one around the back – just myself, miss. Father's away in the city.'

Now she remembered who he was. Will Jenkins, the innkeeper's son. Hadn't he gone to London years ago? Hadn't Fred knocked this savage down more than once when, as little boys, they used to play in the churchyard?

Cassandra hesitated. She must look an absolute sight. It couldn't hurt to try and clean up a little . . .

'Very well, my man,' she said, and followed him with

all the dignity she could muster round the back of the village inn.

He was shorter than Edmund and Fred, but his shoulders were broader for sure, and the linen of his shirt was pale against his sun-browned skin.

He looked back at her over his shoulder. He was smirking, she was certain of it, trying his hardest not to laugh as hard as any of those scruffy children. Cassandra scowled back at him. She thought she would have liked Fred to be here so he could have knocked him down all over again and wiped that smile clear off his face.

The inn was dark inside, and the kitchen, although not unlike the kitchen at Knole Park, in that there was a fire and a large scrubbed table, was a good deal smaller and more cluttered. Herbs hung from the ceiling and the fire glowed red in the grate.

Will Jenkins took a poker and riddled the embers, then put on a couple of logs. 'There, sit yourself down by the fire and dry off, Miss Worrall,' he said. 'If you need some clothes, you could wear mine.'

'Oh, I don't think so, William Jenkins! Some water, please, so I can wash my face, and then I will be off.'

'I didn't mean—' he began, but Cassandra glared at him. 'As you wish.' And he left her alone in the kitchen.

She stood by the fire, unbuttoned her coat and opened it out. The dress underneath was damp, and no doubt she stank of pond weed. She noticed her reflection in the bottom of a copper pan: her golden curls were dishevelled and her face smeared with mud, not unlike the war paint of the Pequot or the Mohican. Edmund would think her ridiculous.

She sighed.

'You are not hurt?'

Cassandra spun round. How long had Will Jenkins been standing there?

'No, I am not.'

'And neither is Zephyr.'

'How do you know my horse's name?'

'Stephen, the lad who works in your stables with Vaughan – he's brought him down to be shod more than once. The animal's a stunner.' Will put a basin of water and a bar of home-made soap down on the table. 'I only ever saw one as fine as him, and that was in London.'

'Really?' Cassandra sat down by the bowl and began to wash.

'A mare – Arab, I'm certain, a blue roan; it was on its way to Paris to race.' He crossed his arms and stared into space. 'I wouldn't have minded going with it – on that boat to Paris, I mean. Although saying that, I'd rather America.'

Cassandra stopped and sat up; she wiped her face and looked at him. Will was in a kind of reverie.

She had never imagined that people like him might think of travel; not in the way that she or Edmund would.

'You?'

'Don't mock me, Miss Worrall! I would've done too if Father hadn't called me back. Would be there right now, riding west . . .'

'I wasn't mocking.' She checked the cloth he'd given her to dry her face.

'It is clean, miss.'

Cassandra blushed. 'Yes, of course, I—'

He leaned forward and looked straight at her, his voice low and deep and gentle. 'In America, Miss Worrall, there ent lords and ladies or gentry or nothing. A working man may look at a lady, such as yourself, and—'

Cassandra realized she couldn't look away. His eyelashes were so dark and long.

There was a loud thump from the saloon, and then Cassandra heard several smaller faster ones. Will Jenkins turned and left the room; she watched him go, suddenly realizing that the smaller thuds were her heart beating fast against her ribcage. She swallowed hard.

How could it be, she wondered, that he had changed so? He could not have been gone long, now that she thought about it, but how had she not noticed him when he first returned? Why had she not seen straight

away that he was – there was no other word for it –
delicious . . . ?

She had not quite dried off when she realized that
there was a commotion in the inn proper, quite jarring
her out of her thoughts. Was there some sort of brawl?
she wondered with a sudden turn to her stomach. She
had not wanted to leave with her dress and hair still wet,
but she didn't want to linger here if something like that
was happening on the other side of that door.

Just then the door burst open again – it was Will, and
he looked quite distracted.

Cassandra gasped. 'Has there been a fight?'

He looked at her as if she had spoken to him in
Dutch. 'No, Miss Worrall,' he said. 'It's this foreign girl,
come in off the Bristol road.'

'Foreign?'

'Definitely foreign, miss – well, perhaps you'd better
see for yourself,' and he took up the bottle of sherry
he had presumably come through for, and left the door
open for her to follow.

She paused. Being a young lady, she had never in all
her years set foot inside the inn itself. But she was already
in the kitchen, wasn't she? She took a deep breath and
drew herself up, imperious despite her bedraggled hair
– she was a Worrall, after all – and stepped across the
threshold, into the ale-brown darkness of the inn.

No one looked her way. All eyes – and more and more people were trickling in – were fixed on the small girl sitting at the long wooden table being questioned by Parson Davies. Her hair seemed to be piled up on her head, but as Cassandra got closer she saw that it was a turban – like the people in India wore in Mama's books. Her dress was made of some kind of black stuff – not satin or silk, but a plain, dull cloth – though fashionably high waisted. It was certainly an English dress, an everyday sort of dress such as Rachel, the parson's help, might wear on a Sunday, if she were in mourning. It was cut high at the front and very modest, and the sleeves were short and puffed. The girl's arms were the same shade as her face, a warm coffee brown – more than the colour that resulted from outdoor work, Cassandra thought – and anyway, the manner in which the girl held herself spoke of something refined.

There was nothing refined about the parson. He was speaking French very, very loudly.

'*Parlez-vous français, mademoiselle?*'

'Does she speak no English?' Cassandra said.

Parson Davies looked at her witheringly.

Will came out from behind the counter with a glass of sherry – Cassandra could smell it, sweet and heady. He addressed her, one hand sweeping that thick dark hair up and away from his face.

'She won't touch a thing, Miss Worrall, and by the looks of her she's quite parched.'

Cassandra had to look away quickly in case she blushed. She found the girl studying her, wide-eyed. Her lips, though full, were cracked and dry.

'I think you are right, Mr Jenkins,' she said, doing her best to sound authoritative.

'I don't think she's northern European . . .' The parson took a deep breath. '*Sprechen Sie Deutsch, Fräulein?*' He reached out and raised her chin so that he could look directly into her eyes, but she was obviously uncomfortable with such intimacy, and shrank from his touch. Then she looked straight at Cassandra, who was struck by her large dark eyes and, as she smiled, her small, even teeth. She was, Cassandra thought, rare pretty.

Will poured the girl some sherry. She wrinkled her pretty nose and pushed it away.

'She must drink something.' Cassandra looked at the girl again and mimed drinking. The girl gazed back, smiling and acting the same mime.

Will shook his head. 'We've tried everything: ale, wine, cider cup.'

'Why don't you simply fetch her some water?' Cassandra said, looking up at him. He held her gaze for an instant and she looked away again; she couldn't help smiling, though – she had felt it as clearly as if it were tangible. There was something between them. She had not conjured it up, or imagined it. It was real. Cassandra nearly gasped with the shock and the pleasure of it. She had not felt like this since the New Year's Ball, when she'd danced with Edmund Gresham . . .

Will returned with a large jug of water. The girl's face brightened, and before he could pour it, she shooed him away. The company watched as she swilled the cup around carefully, holding it up and examining it, making sure that it was spotless. Then she began what looked like prayers, her mouth moving quickly and in a tongue Cassandra had never heard. She made some odd salute and bowed her head, then poured the water out into her cup and drank and drank and drank.

She looked from Cassandra to Will and nodded, saying a single word – it could have been nonsense but the meaning was clear: it was a thank you.

'That might be Italian,' the parson said. 'I don't have any Italian myself . . .'

Cassandra watched as the girl finished the whole pitcher of water, and realized that everyone else was gazing at her too, like visitors staring at a lion or a giraffe in a menagerie.

When the girl had finished, she took a napkin from a small bag she carried at her waist and dabbed her mouth dry in the daintiest manner imaginable.

'What pretty manners! If she's a vagrant then I'm a Chinaman!' a man said – the carter, Cassandra thought; she didn't know his name. 'I'm telling you, Parson, there's something about this girl . . .'

'I'm inclined to agree. Those are not the actions of a beggar.' The parson shook his head. 'Fascinating! Quite, quite fascinating! A most *interesting* maid. The shape of her face! The colour of her skin! Like the best Javan coffee, don't you think?'

The girl looked from one man to the other and then back to Cassandra. She pressed her two palms together as though in prayer, and then placed them at the side of her face, inclined her head and shut her eyes, like a child at bed time.

'She's tired!' the parson said, as if he had discovered the West Indies. 'We ought to take her to the Parish Council. They'll know what to do with her.'

'Parish Council! Pardon, Parson, but you and I know there'll be talk and talk, and then, after a day and a night of talking they'll only send the poor mite to the poorhouse in Bristol,' said the carter. 'And a girl like this'll be broken in two in such a place.'

'But we can't have her here; we've the London stage-coach passing through here this afternoon, and they'll be wanting every bed we have,' Will said.

'And anyway,' the parson added, 'it wouldn't be

proper, what with Mr Jenkins being away and no woman in the house.' He turned to Cassandra. 'Your father would know what to do, Miss Worrall.'

She stood up. Father would have sent the girl to the Bristol poorhouse with a snap of his fingers. He wasn't one for mysteries – just figures and trade and making money, plain and simple. Mama, however, would be most delighted by this stray.

Cassandra held herself tall; she was, in her parents' absence, the lady of the manor. 'I could take her back to Knole Park. Papa's steward, Mr Finiefs, speaks Greek and Persian. Do you think she may be Eastern?'

'Well thought, Miss Worrall!' the parson said. 'She's dark enough.'

The girl yawned – a touch theatrically, Cassandra thought.

'Yes, of course, she is exhausted. You poor, poor thing.'

The girl's eyes were wide and dark and fringed by long thick lashes. She blinked and smiled, but there was no flicker of understanding at all.

'I will take her back with me at once – she can wash and dress and rest. And the Parish Council may make their decison later.'

Cassandra reached out for the girl's hand. 'Come with me. Please.' She tried to speak softly, the way she talked to Zephyr if she didn't want to spook him, but the girl didn't understand at all. 'Come with me, and sleep?' Cassandra mimed sleep with her head on her hands just like the girl had. 'Sleep?'

The girl stood up and took her hand.

'I may need help.' Cassandra looked around the inn as if the thought had only now sprung into her head. Parson Davies stood up but she ignored him. 'William?' She nodded haughtily, suppressing a smile. 'You may accompany us to Knole Park.'

2

EDEN'S RETREAT

Eden's Retreat Posture Club
Strutton Ground
Westminster
April 1819

The girl on the silver tray was utterly naked save for a fish tail, made of papier-mâché, gauze and tinsel. In the flickering glow of yellow candlelight it appeared real enough if anyone looked closely. But of course, given her powdered breasts and rouged nipples, nobody was.

The mermaid stared somewhere off into the distance and kept supremely and completely still. Her hair was as flatly yellow as laburnum flowers. The tray she reclined on was carried at shoulder height by two heavies who negotiated the space around the tables in the back room of the tavern with ease.

The place was full to bursting: a couple of old

gentlemen who had forgotten that wigs had gone out of fashion sat in the corner, but it was mostly young bucks with more cash than sense. Behind the bar, Mrs Ingrams, the owner of the establishment, lit a pipe and smiled as she thought of her takings.

At a table near the stage, three scholars, soon to finish at Westminster School, drank brandy as if it were water.

'Do you think they'll have places like this in Oxford?' George Farringdon could barely keep still. It was his first visit, and in all his seventeen years the only time he had ever set eyes on a girl, a real flesh-and-blood girl, naked. His eyes were practically popping out of their sockets.

Edmund Gresham and Frederick Worrall, regular visitors, exchanged vaguely amused looks.

'I should say so, George,' Edmund said. 'There are places like this everywhere – if one knows where to look.'

'So which one's your Letty?' asked George.

'She's hardly *my* Letty.' Frederick drained his brandy glass. 'Ed's had her as often as I have. In fact, it was Ed who had her first, wasn't it?'

Edmund Gresham ground what remained of one of his father's best Havana cigars into the floor. 'First, I grant you, but you've had her more than me, Fred; many times more! You must have lost count. And anyway, she *is* your Letty. The girl doesn't just carry a torch for you, it's more like a bloody brazier!' He leaned closer to George and said in a kind of stage whisper, 'She does it with Fred for nothing!'

Frederick Worrall lent back in his chair and blew a perfect circle of smoke up into the air. 'It's a gift. The ladies love me – what can I do?'

'Speak of the devil,' Edmund said as a second girl was brought in, long red hair curling down over her naked shoulders, nipples rouged, a kind of gauzy silver scarf around her waist. She was all pink and white curves.

'That's her? What a smasher!' George's eyes were huge; he was practically drooling.

'Well, George, my friend, you can have her. She is all yours – at least while you've cash in your pocket. A couple of shillings and she'll do anything you like,' Fred said.

'Anything?'

Edmund nodded. 'It's in their nature. They're a breed apart.'

'She is looking at you!' George nudged Fred so hard he nearly spilled his brandy.

Fred sighed. 'I wish she wouldn't.'

Edmund explained. 'What he means, George, is that she's in love with him. Arse over tit.'

'And that is a problem?' George made a face and

looked from Edmund to Fred. 'How exactly is that a problem?'

'She wants me to buy her out of here. She doesn't want to be a tart any more. She expects me to buy her off Mrs Ingrams, then find her rooms, pay for her clothes, set her up as a respectable young lady – hah! Even – in her rose-tinted daydreams – marry her! Which of course I'd never do, even if my allowance did stretch to my very own trollop. Thank God term's nearly over – very soon I'll never have to see the little minx again.'

'You two aren't coming back after Easter, then?' George said, not taking his eyes from the girl.

Edmund shook his head. 'School is done. No masters for me. I shall traverse the globe like a Titan.'

Fred made a face. 'I won't be returning. Election term without Edmund? I shall have to suffer several weeks with my people, though. Which will be dull as hell.'

'Surely not!' Edmund said. He turned to George. 'I do believe our Fred is making much of nothing. Knole Park is a riot. There is the beautiful Cassandra – most diverting – and your mother, Fred – she always has some wild scheme. Last Christmas she had us all dress up in Chinese clothes to celebrate the new drawing room! You had a pigtail, as I remember! Why, I do believe your mother is one of a kind. I say, George, if you want some free entertainment you should hear Fred's mother talk!' Edmund put on an approximation of an American accent: 'Nice to meet yeeewwww!'

'Your ma's American?' George asked.

'I'd rather not think of Mama in here, thank you.' Fred lit a cigar. 'You will visit, Edmund? It will be utterly tedious without you. No company to speak of and only the prospect of some decent dances and pretty girls in Bath once the season starts.'

'You'll be taking a house this year?' Edmund asked.

'Papa has promised. My only consolation in a future that promises university and a lifetime of drudgery at the bank.'

George sighed. 'Bath. I hope to go one day. There is a boy in my Greek class who says Bath is a riot.'

Edmund nodded. 'Bath is my favourite place. So many amenable girls. Fred'll be fighting them off with a stick! Your sister – will she be there?'

'If you try anything on with Cass, you know I'll knock you down.'

Edmund smirked. 'And there was me thinking I'd like to see your little sister tricked out in nothing but a silk scarf—'

'Edmund!' Fred scowled.

His friend put his hands up. 'I admit it, I'd marry her tomorrow. Cassandra is a peach, a peach of the first and most supreme order! Fred, I swear on the good book

I'd happily behave and she'd be Lady Gresham and have as many new frocks as her beautiful heart desired.'

'You better behave around Cass, Ed, or I swear you'll end up with fewer teeth in your head than God gave you.'

'Fred! I am only teasing. But the truth is, she couldn't do better than me.'

Fred bristled slightly. 'Possibly. Problem is, I know what you're like. You'd soon grow bored of a wife.'

'And you wouldn't? Fred, that's nature's way. Cassandra would bear me a couple of sons, at least half as handsome as the Worralls, and we'd be brothers! Brothers, Fred!' Edmund smiled. 'You know, old chap, I can't see a rosier future.' He refilled Fred's glass. 'A toast to beauty, and to your lovely sister.' They clinked glasses just as another girl was carried in. 'And who in heaven's name is *that*?'

All heads had turned as a small dark-haired girl with long slender limbs and wearing nothing but a pair of wings was carried in. But instead of blankly staring straight ahead like the other girls, she seemed nervous, even scared. Fred saw her hands shaking and there was a hint of redness around the eyes.

'New, if I'm not mistaken,' Edmund said, leaning forward to get a clearer look.

'Variety is the spice of life.' Fred couldn't take his eyes off the girl.

'Oi! I saw her first!'

'Ah, but you're saving yourself for my sister.' Fred smiled. 'And she does look most deliciously *fresh* . . .'

Fred Worrall examined himself in the looking glass above the wash basin. He was a catch, even though he said it himself: dark blue eyes that looked as free of sin as a summer's day, hair nearly as golden as his sister's, and tall enough to have to watch out he didn't brush the ceilings in these old buildings. He studied himself and frowned: had his looks failed him last night? The girl in the bed made a noise in her sleep and rolled over.

He finished washing. The church bells were ringing for seven and he would be in trouble if he didn't return home over Easter. He had decided to travel with Edmund as far as Gresham Hall and spend a few days there before going on to Knole Park.

Edmund would be on the Newbury coach, which left from the Swan with Two Necks by St Martin in the Fields in an hour. He looked at the girl, her dark hair spilling over the pillows. She opened her eyes, startled, pulling the sheets up over her nakedness.

He would try some tenderness; there was, after all, still time to make it an interesting morning.

'You are a stunner, Betsy, a peach,' Fred said, sitting on the bed. 'The moment I saw you—'

'My name's Essie, sir.'

Fred leaned close. Her face was a perfect heart shape, and he could just make out the shape of her breasts under the sheets, small and perfect. 'I won't hurt you. I promise.'

The girl backed away and gasped, but in terror rather than delight, and clamped her legs hard against his hand.

He pulled away. 'For pity's sake, Betsy! You might try and enjoy it a little!'

'It's Essie, sir,' she squeaked.

Fred saw that her eyes were full of tears. He might have been holding a knife to her neck rather than seducing her.

'Essie! Bessie! I don't give a fig for your damn name!'

'No, sir.'

Fred stood up. 'You could do a lot worse than me. Next time it'll be some toothless old sot with no hair on his head – and the pox, I don't doubt.'

'Yes, sir.' Her voice was trembling.

Fred rolled his eyes. 'I have paid for you, Bessie. Look at me. Do I disgust you? Could you really not bring yourself to kiss me? Would that be such a hardship?'

'I do not know, sir.'

'My name is Fred, not sir!'

The girl sniffed. 'I wanted to be a dancer, sir. I'm good at dancing!' She looked at him, the bedsheet held up to her chin, bottom lip wobbly with grief. He felt his passion cool as surely as if a jug of cold water had been emptied upon him.

'You'll not tell Mrs Ingrams, will you, sir?'

'So you can part another patsy from his cash tonight?'

The girl sobbed all the more.

Fred sighed. He almost sat down on the bed but remembered that his proximity only upset the poor scrap. 'I will not speak of this. I have a reputation of my own. If Edmund found out—'

'Thank you! Oh, sir, thank you!'

Fred turned away and began to dress. He would not tell Edmund about this debacle; his friend would only laugh and say he ought to have taken her no matter what. Fred stole a glance at the girl in the bed. She was wiping her tears with the bedsheet. *Did she not understand her lot?* he wondered.

Fred decided to get to the inn early and take some coffee before the coach left. He thought about Oxford: he was planning to persuade Father to let him do the tour before his studies. Edmund was so lucky – he had it mapped out: Italy, Greece, perhaps even Turkey. Fred could hardly think of anything better. The shine was definitely off London as far as he was concerned. And foreign girls were supposed to be something very special, weren't they? It was a shame Father viewed a tour as a waste of time, merely a chance to put off employment.

Fred thought of the prospect of weeks at Knole Park – weeks that would stretch out into a lifetime if he wasn't careful. Mother would ask about the books he'd read – none – and Father would talk about banks and stocks and shares, and Cass would try and interest him in her equally silly friend Diana Edgecombe.

He sighed. He hoped there'd be a chance to escape for some sport. He turned to the girl again, but she simply looked away.

Fred had put his breeches on and was buttoning his shirt when there was a commotion on the stairs and the door flew open.

'Letty!' Fred grinned, then glanced at his pocket watch on the bedside table. 'I am so pleased to see you!' His mind ran ahead and he stopped doing up his shirt. There was still a good half-hour—

Letty strode in and slapped him hard across his face. The sting was not quite as shocking as the fact of the blow.

'Ow.' Fred put a hand to his face. 'Ow! Letty, are you completely mad?' She looked dishevelled, her hair unpinned and her silk gown a little grubby in the morning sunlight.

'Only 'cause you made me so!' She made to hit him again, but Fred caught her hand.

'Letty!' He would be firm with her. 'Letty, I will have words with Mrs Ingrams. Stop this now!'

Letty dissolved in a pool of tears. 'Please, sir! No, sir!'

Fred threw her off him. 'Lord! Not you too! Are tears contagious?'

'No, Mr Fred, my love, my darling. Please, Freddie, I am sorry. Forgive me – I was driven to it! I never meant to hurt you, honest to God. I do so love you, my own, my love!'

'Well, don't go slapping me about the face again, there's a good girl.'

Letty took a deep breath in through her tears. 'I love you!'

'No you don't, Letty.' Fred smiled at the girl in the bed, who was looking on, mesmerized.

'She won't be no good for you, that one!' Letty pointed at her.

'I think I know that now, but if you will get out of my way, I do have a coach to catch.' Fred fastened his cuffs and took down his jacket from the back of the door.

'Don't leave me! Mr Fred, please! You said you loved me – you said I was your own, your special one!' Letty was wailing, her face wet with tears.

'Letty, don't be a bore. I have to go.'

'But you promised me . . .' She threw herself at his

feet, holding onto his legs. 'You promised me there weren't no other!'

'I promised you nothing of the sort, Letty. Ever. I am leaving. Let me go, woman!' He practically had to kick her away.

'But the child, Mr Fred! Our child!' She lay on the floor, sobbing. 'I won't be able to work no more and you promised me – you said you'd buy me out of Eden's!'

Fred hid a flash of fear. 'Do you think me soft in the head? The old "child" lay? Edmund warned me about this. That child could have ten fathers as soon as blink.'

Letty wailed again. 'It's yours, sir. It's yours, I knows it! And all those words, Mr Fred – you said I was yours. You *said*!'

'We had some fun, Letty, don't go spoiling it.' Fred retrieved his hat and put it on, checking his reflection in the looking glass.

Letty was still crying inconsolably. 'You have broke me, Mr Fred, you surely have!' She went to the window. 'I shall throw myself out, myself and the baby! I shall die flat on the pavement like Polly Marsden, all the blood seeped out of me!'

Fred froze. He had been there, with Letty, when it happened. He had never seen anything so vile in all his life.

'For God's sake, Letty!' He grabbed her wrist with

one hand, and with the other reached deep into his pocket and fished out half a crown. 'There.' He pressed it into her hand. 'Better now?'

Letty stared at the money then looked at him. She stepped down off the window seat and cursed him. 'You are a bastard in all but name, Mr Fred, an' that's the truth.'

'Letty, I am leaving, and that's an end to it.'

Her face turned murderous. 'You are rotten inside and no mistake.' She came closer to him. 'There is no baby! And if there was I'd kill it three times over if it was yours.'

Fred stared at her. 'I knew it! Edmund was right, you girls are all liars—'

'I never loved any of it, not one single second. I only loved your money.'

'Yes, well, that's the lot of a trollop—'

'Mr Fred, you don't know nothing about love and you never will. Your heart is dead and rotten – if you have a heart at all!'

Fred opened the door. 'So please leave. I have a stage to catch.'

Letty didn't move.

He sighed. 'What is it you want now?'

'From you?' She looked at him with utter contempt and swore, her words dripping venom.

'How dare you speak to me like that? You girls need to remember how to treat your betters.'

'Betters? You! You are a disease that walks on two legs! You wouldn't know how to make a girl love you unless you gave her cash up front, and you never will.' She started laughing at him, then sat down on the bed, almost hysterical.

He shouted down the stairs: 'Mrs Ingrams!' He shouted louder. 'Mrs Ingrams! Come at once! Letty is having a turn.' Then he tipped his hat at the girl in the bed and left.

The coach journey was long and uncomfortable, and not, which was a new feeling entirely, just physically. Fred tried to sleep as the coach bumped and jolted along the rutted conduits that passed for roads, but he could not stop thinking about what Letty had said. However hard he pushed the memory away, she came back, laughing at him, telling him he didn't know anything about love.

How ridiculous was that? What in heaven's name could a girl like Letty know about love?

And what did she know about *him*? Nothing, that's what. Absolutely nothing. Of course, when he married, it would be for love, not simply some commercial transaction. He would love someone – some girl, some pure and decent maid – and she would love him back.

Wouldn't she?

What did love feel like when you hadn't paid for it?

He couldn't sleep.

Letty was jealous. Love was not for trollops and tarts. Everyone knew that.

3

THE PRINCESS CARABOO

Knole Park House
April 1819

The Princess woke suddenly, gasping for air. For a second it felt as if she was fighting for breath.

Perhaps she was dead already, drowned in rotting leaves and cherry blossom. Then she opened her eyes and all she could see was white; shining, clean, burning white. This was death, surely.

Once her eyes became used to the light, she saw that she was in a small whitewashed room. Yellow sunlight flooded in through the square window and bounced off the white walls, the white sheets, the white rug.

'Miss? Miss!' A girl was shaking her shoulder.

The Princess knew she could not be dead, unless the angels in heaven went about their business dressed as housemaids.

Suddenly it all came back. The burning thirst on the road; the collapse – she must have collapsed; the inn, dark and stinking of ale; and the ride in the cart to this big house. It looked old, not one of the smart white stuccoed houses of London or Marlborough. This one was brick built, with a castle turret stuck on one side which looked as out of place as a girl wearing a summer straw hat in the rain. It was not a castle, the daughter of the house had explained when she saw her looking. It was, she said, waving her hand, nothing more than a kind of fancy.

Her old self had seen grand houses before – in Exeter and in London, when she had worked as a nanny for families of quality. Indeed, she thought, the people she had worked for in London had finer paintings, but she had never seen anything like the drawing room the pretty blonde girl – Cassandra, that was her name – had led her into . . .

The wallpaper was pink – rosy, precious pink like the clouds at sunrise – with blue flowers and birds, that striking clear blue of high summer skies. She had looked around and her mouth must have fallen open like the worst sort of village idiot, but Cassandra merely steered her to a chair.

'Mama! Mama!' she had called, and a woman of middle age, hurried in, untying her bonnet, closely followed by a tired-looking gentleman.

The woman clapped her hands. 'This is the girl? Oh my!'

The man harrumphed. He was still wearing his fine travelling cloak. 'Finiefs! Bless my soul, where is the man?'

'Mr Worrall – Samuel.' The woman came close and stared at the girl in the chair, ignoring the black gown, covered with dust from the road. She looked at her face. 'They found her at the inn, Cassandra?'

'Yes, Mama. She speaks no English, not a word.'

The man, Mr Worrall, harrumphed again. 'She is a beggar – Bristol is crawling with them. I will get Finiefs or Vaughan to take her to the workhouse in the city. See the dust she is trailing! I did not pay a sultan's ransom for your Chinese drawing room to be filled with filthy foreign beggars who might be crawling with vermin and have an eye to steal whatever we have!'

'Father!'

In the chair the girl made no move. Whatever anyone said about her, she would not let it show. Nothing could hurt her any more. Not after her heart had been broken, her baby dead and her body ruined. She would be a princess now, a princess who knew nothing of pain and sadness. She was new; she was spotless. She sat taller in the chair and regarded the man, the woman and the girl with the same intensity as they regarded her.

'Perhaps we should take her into the library, Cassandra.'

'Take her away, more like.' The man opened the door and yelled into the house, 'Finiefs! Dammit, man, I don't pay you to sit upon your—'

Suddenly a man in servant's livery came into the room. He was puffing with exertion.

Mr Worrall nodded. 'Ah, Mr Finiefs.'

The black-haired man dipped in a bow. 'Sir?'

'I want this girl on the trap and back to the Bristol poorhouse.'

The girl in the chair smiled as if this meant nothing, as if she had never heard the word and had no idea what the thing was. After all, the person she was now had never spent a night in such a place. Ever.

'Papa! Please,' Cassandra begged.

'Yes, Samuel, one night, let her stay one night,' Mrs Worrall said. 'I should like to hear her speak – they had no idea of her language?'

Cassandra shook her head. 'And, Mama, you should have seen her when she saw this room. I do believe it means something to her . . .'

'Take her through to the library.' Mrs Worrall opened the door; her husband made a face. 'Samuel, please. This is a chance to study someone at close quarters. She is most interesting, it is clear.'

'She is a foreign beggar! In Bristol we have Negro beggars, Lascar beggars – Mr Finiefs, I wager, in Athens or wherever you were born, the beggars are as dark as this one.'

'Oh, darker indeed, sir, madam.'

Cassandra had taken the girl's hand. 'Come,' she said, and led her back across the marble tiled hall and into the library.

If the Chinese drawing room had been a source of wonder, the library, with its rows and rows of books, had been a revelation. Of course she could read. Every year she had won an orange at Sunday school in the Primitive Baptist chapel in Witheridge for her knowledge of the scriptures. Where had her first stories come from? All those stories of marvels and enchantment? And here were more books than she had ever seen in all her seventeen years. And weren't stories more rewarding than life? Stories had never let her down, had never promised anything they did not deliver.

She and Peg had shared a bed above their father's workshop. Peg was scared of everything: she shied at thunderstorms, owls, the cries of foxes, and she had told her tales – of princesses riding across mountains on white horses, warrior maids fighting dragons, unicorns and leopards. Princesses who could hunt and fish, swim and climb, relying on no one but themselves.

'Mama does love books,' Cassandra whispered.

The Princess remembered where and who she was. A story made flesh. She must not forget.

The adults were bickering now. Mr Worrall was close to winning. The Princess thought that if she did not take her future in hand she would be sleeping on the floor of the women's derelicts ward in the Bristol poorhouse.

She let go of Cassandra and turned and faced Mrs Worrall. One thing she had learned was that servants never looked straight at their superiors, never met their eyes. That was for equals. But wasn't she a princess now? She was better than the whole room of them. She must not avert her eyes.

The Princess saluted, looked Mrs Worrall straight in the eye and smiled. She summoned up all those old languages she had ever heard – on the London streets, in the hedgerows near the Romany camps she'd spied on with her sister. She saluted again. '*Inju jagoos!*' she said. '*Inju jagoos, Lazor*' – she nodded at Mrs Worrall and her daughter – '*Manjinttoo*' – she nodded at Mr Worrall – '*Makrittoos*' – and finally at Mr Finiefs.

Mrs Worrall gasped. 'Oh my, Samuel! I do believe she is something very special!' She looked at Finiefs. 'Get Phoebe to make up a bed – until we know who she is she will stay.'

Mr Worrall had harrumphed once more.

She'd had to do her best not to smile too widely.

She sat up slowly. Judging by the light it must be late. How long had she slept? The sheets were cool crisp linen that felt as exotic as the finest oriental silks. No, she reminded herself, she was a princess – this was surely the very least she would be used to. She watched the maid's back as she bent low over the fireplace and swept up the ashes.

What would happen if she was discovered? What if this girl could see right through her? What if they all did? She looked for the black gown – if they had taken it away, how would she ever leave? Would she have to run all the way to the city in a borrowed nightgown? She must calm down. No one would know. If she acted like a princess, then that is what they would all see. And the lady of the house certainly wanted her to be real – one of those books in the library come to life, a walking, talking, breathing native for her to study. If she could only keep her nerve, she thought, she might even play the royal savage until luncheon.

She realized the maid was staring.

'Have no fear, miss!' the girl said. 'It's only, me, Phoebe, remember? Phoe-be.' She spoke slowly and put her hand, red raw from work, on the Princess's brow.

'You might be ailing . . . are you ailing? You ent starting a fever, so that's something . . .'

The Princess nodded benignly at the maid.

Suddenly there was a commotion on the stair outside and Mr Finiefs the steward burst unbidden into the room. He looked around; the Princess saw his eyes fall on her, and it wasn't until then that he began yelling in his foreign accent and pointing out of the room. 'Fire! Fire! Quick! The west stairs!'

The Princess saw the colour drain from Phoebe's cheeks instantaneously, as if the blood had suddenly stopped pumping. Her hand flew to her mouth. 'Oh Lor'!' she said, and fled.

It was quite fascinating, the Princess thought, how easily folk could be taken in – by love, or other much simpler lies. She herself did not move, but blinked slowly at Mr Finiefs and listened as Phoebe hurtled away down the stairs.

'There's a fire! Now! We must leave! We'll all be burned alive!' Mr Finiefs was still shouting and doing his best to look agitated.

The Princess cocked her head to one side but did not get out of bed. She knew what he was doing. She was not that stupid.

Mr Finiefs looked over his shoulder – checking that Phoebe had gone, the Princess thought – and came closer. She was not scared: he might be a man, but he was old and, more importantly, a servant. She stared back at him imperiously. She imagined she was sitting on a throne, a boy with a fan wafting cooling breezes over her, a leopard – or even better, a unicorn – curled at her feet. Now that he was close, she could see his yellow teeth, and the lines in his forehead were deeper than winter ploughing in a heavy clay field. As he spoke, spittle flew in silver droplets towards her face. He was a mere steward. She would not flinch.

I expect, she said in her head, *you miss your homeland. Well, I do too.* She raised an eyebrow.

Mr Finiefs rolled his eyes. 'Give it a rest, girl. You won't take me in by jabbering nonsense and putting on a show. Looking for charity, I expect.'

The Princess only smiled.

Mr Finiefs paced about the room, then came to rest by the window. When he spoke again, his voice was cruel, sharp. 'Look, I don't know who you are but know this: I am watching you like a hawk. Remember that – like a *hawk*!' He folded his arms. 'The master is not a fool. He has not taken kindly to you and your pig Latin. The mistress and Miss Cassandra might have soft hearts, but I assure you mine is carved from hardest Grecian marble.'

The Princess looked at Mr Finiefs and made up

her mind she would depart after breakfast. There was no reason to stay once she had washed and eaten. Breakfast! Her stomach rumbled in a markedly unregal manner and she smoothed the bed linen across her lap. She imagined bread and warm milk . . . but perhaps princesses only ate pigeon, or trout freshly caught from royal fishponds. Perhaps this princess only ate food she caught herself – she was, after all, a warrior. She would have to think on that.

Mr Finiefs was still talking. 'The Worralls are good people, and if you have plots or plans against them, I swear I will make you suffer!'

The Princess did not flinch. She would have liked to tell him he needn't worry, that she would be back on the road and would leave his precious Worralls well alone. But she doubted he would have believed her.

Her stomach rumbled again. Oh for a cup of tea! The Princess thought she would give her entire kingdom for one small cup of tea.

At that moment Phoebe came back with Miss Cassandra. Phoebe was almost jumping up and down with delight.

'See, Miss Cassandra! Mr Finiefs came in yelling "Fire!" and she didn't move an inch. Nothing showed on her face, nothing at all!'

The Princess kept the serene smile in place.

'This is true?' Cassandra asked Mr Finiefs, although it was obvious to the whole room that she had already made up her mind.

He sighed and made a little shrugging gesture. Cassandra clapped her hands and approached the Princess. Her eyes shone with almost the same intensity that she had turned on the boy from the inn yesterday. And the Princess had seen the boy look back at her the same way. He would break her heart, the Princess thought, or perhaps she would break his. She remembered Robert – the father of her child, the young man who had made her forget herself – and blinked. Robert Lloyd had worked in a dairy close to the Borough. He had the loveliest, darkest, most honest eyes she had ever seen; he called her *cariad* and promised her marriage, and she had believed him; believed him with all her heart – until she had discovered she was pregnant, and he had found another girl quick as blinking.

Her heart was broken – though she forced herself to watch through the window as Jenny Pierce sat behind the counter in the Lloyds' shop and showed off her wedding band like a queen.

The Princess reminded herself never, ever to fall in love. Cassandra had no idea. It would end in tears or worse; love always did.

Cassandra sat down on the bed. She placed her hand

over her heart. 'Cass-andra . . .' She spoke slowly and seriously and said it again. 'Cass-andra.'

Then she pointed at the Princess. The Princess paused for a long second. She was thinking about her name. Her name would have to be incredible. The Princess was a warrior, a noblewoman; no, she was more than that – she was from another world.

The Princess looked around the room. All eyes were on her – Phoebe expectant, Mr Finiefs pretending indifference. The Princess slowly and deliberately lifted her own hand up to her heart and half closed her eyes. 'Car–a–boo,' she said. 'Car–a–boo.'

Some days later the Princess Caraboo lay flat on her front against the sun-warmed tiles of the roof of the west wing of Knole Park. She was dressed in one of Miss Cassandra's cast-off Indian muslins, though cut short and adapted into suitable warrior princess mode, the excess fabric wound around her head as a turban, a strip tied around her waist as a belt, with a small sharp knife she had taken from the kitchen tucked into it. She was very proud of her bow and arrows. She had made them the day before when Cassandra gave her a tour of the grounds.

Cassandra had taken great care, leading her around the stables and the gardens, and along the avenue of tall trees that waved carefree in the breeze. Caraboo had sprinted barefoot across the drive and up into a tree.

For a moment yesterday afternoon the Princess was gone and she was once again the girl who had been afraid of nothing. The girl who wanted to see the world so badly that one small village could not hold her. That girl had known how to fashion a bow, and Caraboo sat all afternoon sharpening her arrows and holding them up to make sure they were true. This would be their first test.

Very quietly she took an arrow from the quiver on her back and lined it up. She held her breath. A few feet away were two pigeons, the male puffed up and cooing and pouting around a smaller female, who was doing her best to feign disinterest. *How like humans*, the Princess thought, and pulled the bowstring taut, her arrow tip aimed fast upon the bird's heart.

At that moment there was a clatter and a thud as the trapdoor opened and Cassandra popped her blonde head up directly in Caraboo's line of fire. The pigeons flapped noisily away and Caraboo had to stop herself from taking Cassandra's eye out.

'Oh, I say! Oh, I am sorry!' Cassandra clambered up, smoothing out her dress. 'Scared them off, did I?' She stood up straight, looked around and took in the view, one hand shading the sun from her eyes.

'This is marvellous, Caraboo! Absolutely wonderful!' She took a deep breath in. 'I've never been up here before. You can see clean across to the village. If I had Father's glasses I could see right into the yard of the Golden Bowl!'

Cassandra coloured to match the pink flowers on her dress, and even though she had lost the pigeon, Princess Caraboo smiled.

'What do you know, Caraboo?' Cassandra said. 'A lot more than you say, I am sure of it!'

Caraboo titled her head on one side, and pointed at the pigeons, which had flown in a lazy loop away from Knole and then back to the roof of the stable block.

Cassandra turned back in the direction of the village. 'Do you know, my heart burns just to think of him. And try as I might, I cannot help thinking about him; I cannot eat for wanting him!' She looked almost sad, Caraboo thought. 'This is love, I am certain of it. No passing fancy, I am sure as sure,' she went on.

Caraboo had to look away in case she smiled.

Cassandra sighed. 'You have no idea what I am saying, do you? And it's lucky, for I hate to think what Papa would do if he knew. Or Fred.' She sat down next to Caraboo. 'He'll be back soon, my brother. He's nicer than he seems, all bluster and show. He'd knock my Will down if he knew, but Will would surely hit him harder!'

She paused. 'My Will . . . Have you ever felt like that – so completely and utterly belonging to another that you will die without them?'

Caraboo tucked her bow across her shoulder, then reached out and touched Cassandra's arm. *Forget him*, she wanted to say. *Ride your horse as fast as you can, gallop him out of your heart, because he will leave you, or hurt you, or hit you – or, worse, despise you.* But she couldn't.

Cassandra changed the subject. 'We must get you ready for this afternoon. Mama says that a gentleman, a professor from London, is coming to talk to you and wishes to write down your every word. Who knows, perhaps he can talk to you? I know I wish I could.'

Caraboo kept smiling, but cursed inwardly. She was the stupid one – hadn't she meant to leave by now? She could have been far away on the other side of Bristol, four days closer to home, and instead she was still here, playing at princesses.

A professor! What was she thinking?! She should stop this now. She did not want to hurt Cassandra, or Mrs Worrall, who was kindness itself. And even Mr Worrall, who had not taken kindly to her but was always out at the bank in Bristol.

Knole had been so easy – the cool sheets, a bed of her own, three meals a day; and yesterday hadn't she caught her first pigeon? She had plucked and roasted it over a little fire she'd made in the rose garden, Mrs Worrall watching the noble savage at work all the while. It had been too diverting, being the Princess, worshipping the sun, imagining a life far away where her father was King, speaking in tongues like the old ladies in the Primitive Baptist chapel in Witheridge, another lifetime away.

After all, she was Caraboo now, a princess who had stepped new and entire onto the earth upon the Bristol road. That was the whole truth of it, nothing more, nothing less.

So many thoughts chased around inside Caraboo's head. She would have to leave, and soon. She could pick up a cart on the road to Bristol, but she'd need her old clothes back; she couldn't wander around like this. And even if she couldn't keep the bows and arrows, perhaps she would take a knife, just for protection—

No! She would take nothing. She was a princess. She was not a thief. She would leave this house exactly as she had come into it.

'Oh, Caraboo! What shall I do?' Cassandra was about to start up about her Will again. Caraboo wanted to think straight, to make plans, to stop the bees of indecision buzzing around inside her head.

Behind the house the park sloped away towards

a lake, sparkling blue in the sunlight. In the centre Caraboo could see a small island shaped exactly like a comma. She longed to sit upon that island and think.

She took Cassandra's hand. '*Ana!*' she said.

Cassandra smiled. 'Oh, I know that one! That means "water", doesn't it?' She mimed drinking. 'Yes, well, it is rather warm up here.'

Caraboo half nodded and tugged her back to the trapdoor. '*Ana!*' she said.

'*Ana,*' Cassandra said back.

But Caraboo didn't stop when she reached the kitchen: she pulled Cassandra out through the front door and down along the little path to the lake. '*Ana!*' she said, pointing at the water.

Cassandra shrugged. 'You don't want a drink?'

Caraboo laid down her precious bow and arrow. She took the knife she wore at her waist and set it carefully next to them on the grass, then sprang into the water and swam, striking out for the island.

She sat on the island, made a fire, and wrung her dress out to dry by it. She was wondering how to get a dress she could wear on the road home. She cursed in her new language. If only she'd had the foresight to keep the black cotton gown – buried it somewhere instead of allowing Mrs Bridgenorth, the housekeeper, to take it away.

Cassandra had so many: maybe just one would not be stealing? Oh! If only she could be left alone on this island, like a kind of hermit, free to hunt and fish. The water was as good as any high wall . . .

Once it was dark she would make her way back to the house and take one dress, one dress alone, then head quietly across the fields to meet the Bristol road without passing through the village. Perhaps in Bristol she could pick up pennies begging or even find some work and save enough to travel back to Devon from there. Even if Father wouldn't be glad to see her, Peg would, wouldn't she? She blinked away the tears. Peg would be sixteen now. She hoped to God life had been kind to her sister. In her mind's eye she saw the house – two storeys, cob built; Father hard at work at his cobbler's bench. She and Peg would walk along arm in arm, and when she told her tale, her sister's mouth would gape in amazement, her eyes widening like the Worralls' soup dishes, and they would laugh and hug and laugh again.

She sniffed. She was Princess Caraboo. Caraboo did not cry.

For a while she lay on her back in the clearing and wished it was September, when there would be berries to eat. She found a few mushrooms and laid them by the fire to dry. Princesses had no truck with salad, she thought.

Caraboo felt her dress – it was still damp – and noticed that the sun had lowered in the sky. She imagined the professor and Mrs Worrall twiddling their thumbs, but she tried not to feel guilty. She was just putting her dress back on when she heard footsteps, the breaking of twigs – the sound of two people, not one. She felt for her knife and cursed herself for not bringing it with her.

Just then she heard Cassandra's voice, high, excited and relaxed. Whoever was with her made her laugh. Cassandra would not hurt her. Not yet, at least. Perhaps she had brought the professor. Perhaps there was a whole party of visitors.

She didn't have time to climb up a tree and disappear, so she took a deep breath, and tried to look realistically and thoroughly surprised when she noticed Cassandra standing close by with a young man.

But the man who stood next to her, arm in arm, was far too young for a professor. His eyes were the same bright blue as Cassandra's, and although his hair was less glossy, less golden, he was still very fair. She stared at him. Very fair in all ways, in fact.

Caraboo stood up. She was a princess, she reminded herself. She was brave, even without her weapons. The young man looked as if he was about to laugh out loud; then he studied her in the way young men did, pausing over her bare legs.

Caraboo lifted her chin and stared back at him, directly into his bright blue eyes.

So this was Fred Worrall. She could read the arrogance in his face as surely as if it had been printed in letters. Any fairness she had seen was cancelled out by the curl of his lip and the flint-hard edge to his eyes. Caraboo imagined the leopard at her side growling at him.

'There you are!' Cassandra said. 'Mama's professor has not arrived, but we have a much more exciting visitor!' She smiled and hugged the young man on her arm.

'She is fierce, Cass, I grant you that,' he said.

'Oh yes! And a great shot, Fred. She bagged a pigeon yesterday, right through the heart!'

Cassandra was speaking but Caraboo didn't hear her. This young man would not look away, and she was damned if she would be the first one to blink!

'Caraboo,' Cassandra said solemnly, then placed her hand over his heart. 'Fred-er-ick. My brother.'

Caraboo was still staring as imperiously as before. This man would not best her.

Cassandra nudged him and he turned to look at her. Caraboo had won; she allowed herself a smile.

'Oh, Cass!' Fred said, and he was smiling now. 'Do you honestly believe this girl's not playing!'

Cassandra looked piqued. 'She speaks no English, Fred. Look at her! She's not from here at all. Mama reckons she's nobility.'

'Nobility!' He snorted. 'She is nothing but a party turn, a show, she's a – a flatty catcher, we call 'em in town. A beggar, a mort, one step down from a tart, I'll warrant!'

'Fred! No!' At least Cassandra was standing up for her.

'I've seen a dozen girls tricked out better than this dancing in—' He stopped himself and quickly changed the subject. 'Honestly, Cass! Did she not hide herself away from the professor?'

'How could she? She didn't understand that he was coming.'

'She's a trickster! A coney catcher and nothing more.'

'Fred! Don't say that!'

'You said she didn't understand the lingo.'

'Yes, but your tone speaks volumes!' Cassandra hissed.

'Look at her! Mama said she is from the Indies or some such . . . She's from nowhere further than London or Bristol, I'd put money on it! And as to noble . . . She's just some girl from the street! One whose father or grandfather was an African off some boat! An *octaroon*, the word is. If her blood is blue, then I'm a Dutchman!'

He looked at Caraboo as if she were a piece of dirt.

Cassandra looked upset, but Caraboo kept her face blank; she simply stamped out what was left of the fire. *He was despicable!* she thought. *A coney catcher from the street! London or Bristol! He was so wrong!* She looked back at him arguing with his sister, a good foot taller than her. How dare he think she was anything other than a princess?! She scattered the half-dried mushrooms that were to have been her supper and walked away.

Caraboo strode into the lake, the water cooling and shaping her anger into something solid. As she struck out for the lawn, she could hear Cassandra shouting that they had a boat. Ha! Caraboo would never get into a boat with that man in a thousand years.

She knew exactly what she would do. She would show this city braggart; she would make him believe her. She would go back to the house, and as soon as that professor liked, she would find a way to make him tell them the truth about Princess Caraboo.

4

AN EDUCATED OPINION

Knole Park House
April 1819

Fred woke, sharply, from a dream. He had been at
school, in a Latin class, but that wild brown girl Mama
had taken as a pet was whispering in his ear. And
although he could not understand one word, he could
feel the warmth of her breath, and sometimes, perhaps,
the tip of her tongue on his skin.

'Master Frederick!' The door swung open and Fred
turned sideways so as not to alarm whichever of the
housemaids it might be.

Then, just for a second, he remembered Letty wailing
and cursing, and felt something that might have been a
prickle of guilt – but that vanished as soon as he opened
his eyes.

'Good morning, Master Frederick!' It was the

housekeeper, Mrs Bridgenorth, coming in with a tray of coffee and pastries which she set down on the table close to his bed. She drew back the curtains and clapped her hands together, her eyes creasing into crow's feet as she smiled at him. 'It is lovely to have you home, young sir. And oh, my,' she looked him up and down with an almost motherly pride, 'you *have* grown!'

'Fred, darling!' Cassandra breezed in behind Mrs Bridgenorth and sat down on the bed. 'You must come and see!'

'See? What? Cass, this feels like the middle of the night. And anyway, I am not dressed.'

'It is eight already!'

'Eight!' Fred pulled a face.

'She's on her way up to the roof!'

'She?'

'Caraboo!' Cassandra tried to tug the blankets off. 'Come on, Fred! You *have* to see her welcome the sun – it's wonderful!'

'Oh Lord!' He sat up. 'Caraboo. Your new pet will make patsies and fools out of the lot of us.'

'You are such a cynic, Fred.' Cassandra was pouting.

The housekeeper poured out two cups of coffee and put them on the bedside table.

'Bridgenorth?' Fred said as he pulled his dressing gown from the end of the bed and wriggled his arms into the sleeves. 'You are always so sensible. What do you make of Mama's new fancy? This Caraboo – is she all that she seems?'

The housekeeper shook her head and tutted, looking almost amused. 'Cassandra told me you didn't like her, Master Frederick. Well, I think her lovely. In all ways.'

Fred humphed. 'I think the whole household has gone mad. Surely you can see she's playing us all for a load of fools! I worry Mama has the wool pulled down firmly over her eyes. The Worrall name will be mud across the county if we're not careful.'

'But that's why the professor is here!' Cassandra said. 'And Mama has engaged a naval captain too – a gentleman who knows the East Indies better than you know the West End. They will arrive soon, she said.'

'Indeed, Master Frederick, your sister is right.'

'Bridgenorth, please. It is *Mister* Fred. You may have noticed that I am no longer a ten-year-old boy.'

Mrs Bridgenorth bobbed a curtsey. 'Indeed I have, *Mister* Frederick.' Fred frowned a little – he got the impression she was patronising him.

'See!' Cassandra said. 'Bridgenorth agrees with me. Now bring your coffee and come up to the roof. I'll warrant you've never seen anything like this in all your years in London!'

Fred put on his dressing gown and followed

Cassandra up past the schoolroom towards the attics. He hadn't been up here for such a long time.

At the end of a long corridor a ladder had been let down, and the morning sun slanted in through the open trapdoor.

'There!' Cassandra said. 'You go up first. Go quietly, for she may have started.'

Frederick shook his head and climbed up the ladder.

He didn't see Caraboo straight away, in amongst the sloping roofs and chimney pots. He climbed through the trapdoor and looked around. There was a most excellent view all the way down to the Bristol Channel, and even the docks – he could just see a small forest of masts, so far away they could have been toothpicks – and the blue of the water stretching away to the west, the sky arching up overhead. It was breathtaking.

'Can you see her?' Cassandra shouted up.

'No.'

There was a scrabbling noise. A couple of pigeons flew up and Fred inched round the roof to where a flat space opened up towards the back of the house, overlooking the stables. There she was – Caraboo, arms outstretched, sitting on the parapet, legs dangling over the edge. Her hair was unpinned and she was wearing what looked like one of Cassandra's cast-off nightdresses.

The hair and dress billowed, and Fred saw her throw

her arms out wide and put her head on one side.

Not three months ago he had seen Polly Marsden jump from the second floor of Eden's Retreat. A crowd had gathered and he had, to his shame, been stupid and drunk enough to laugh and shout at her as she teetered, weeping, on the window ledge. Mrs Ingrams had been calling her in, Polly wailing all the while that her heart was broken – although how a woman like that could have a heart, Fred could not fathom. But she had jumped, heart or no, and the sound and the sight of the twisted body hitting the roadway had made him sick to his stomach with both horror and shame.

He called to Caraboo, 'Miss! Miss?'

She didn't turn round.

Cassandra, coming up behind him, must have heard the tone of his voice. 'Fred, what is it?'

'Miss, please! Come away now!'

In her right hand Caraboo held a small bunch of pink willow herb. She held one hand out at right angles and let the flowers fall.

'Miss!'

Fred ran forward and grabbed the girl by the shoulders, dragging her away from the edge. For a second he felt his own centre of gravity sway perilously into the wind, and his heart swooped and his stomach tightened. 'There!' he said, as calmly as he could.

Caraboo wasn't in the least grateful, though. Instead, she pulled away from him and started up a stream of angry babble, half directed at Fred, half at Cassandra.

Fred looked at his sister. 'What in the devil's name is she saying! I thought she was going to jump!'

Cassandra was trying to calm Caraboo, making soft shushing sounds and patting her shoulder. Fred looked at the flat roof where the girl had chalked strange symbols; in front of a kind of home-made altar, she had set out a bowl of water, her bow and arrows, and her knife.

'She was sitting on the edge! I thought—!'

'She was praying. And you scared her! Honestly, Fred. She was praying to Allah Tallah.'

'Allah Tallah?'

'Mama thinks that's her god.'

After listening to Cassandra's soothing words, Caraboo gave Fred a look that would have curdled milk, then knelt down on the flat part of the roof facing east.

'Fred, get back,' Cassandra hissed. 'And be quiet. No quick movements.'

'Hah! She gave *me* the scare, not the other way round!' Though Fred was whispering too.

'You shouldn't have touched her. She doesn't like men touching her.'

Fred sneered. 'Tell you that, did she?'

'Shut up, Fred.'

They watched the girl bow down before rising onto her knees again and pressing her raised hands together.

'Allah Tallah!' she intoned seriously. 'Allah Tallah!' She faced the morning sun, which had just risen over the birch wood towards the village. Then she bowed three times, each time taking a deep breath.

'Is that it?' Fred whispered. 'I've seen the Mussulmen in London make more of a show. We had a boy in school, son of a maharajah, who worshipped, of all things, a bright blue elephant.'

'Fred, you are teasing.'

'No, I swear, it's the truth. Edmund ragged him until he got so sore he hit Ed square in the face.'

'I don't believe Edmund would do such a thing.'

'Hah! You do not know him so well, then.'

'Well, perhaps he deserved it.'

'Aha, you *do* have your eye on him, don't you? After all, he has more cash than anyone I know – isn't that the way to a girl's heart? And he's not far from handsome. Girls fight over him almost as much as they fight over me.'

'Well, that just shows you know nothing about girls! Money is nothing without tenderness! Edmund Gresham?' Cass pulled a face. 'I would sooner put out my own eyes with a soup spoon!'

'Aha again! You protest too much! You carry a torch

for the fellow and no mistake. Even when you pretended affection for Thomas Slatherton . . . and then, after that . . . who was it? Yes, I remember! That George Farthing! George Farting, more like! I wonder what happened to him after you threw his heart away so coldly.'

'I did not!'

'Cass, I've never known a girl so fickle! Always! You favour one thing wholeheartedly, and then, sometimes the following day, another! Remember, when you were small, that doll – Amelia? She was loved and hated, turn and turnabout. Your heart has a different favourite every school holiday. I pity those you pin your affections on, really I do.'

'And you, Fred, are Sir Constant!'

'I am a man; the rules are different.' Fred smiled. 'Admit it – you and Edmund.'

Cassandra had gone pale with fury. 'Why are the rules different, Fred? Tell me that! I wouldn't have your Edmund if he was the last man alive. He is arrogant and so full of his own importance he might burst. He knows nothing of the world. I doubt he has ever done a day's honest toil in his life!' She turned to look at her brother. 'In fact you two are alike in, oh, so many ways. You know only of London fancies and nothing of the soil, of real existence . . .' She got up and turned to look at Caraboo, but the Princess had gone.

'The soil?' Fred shook his head. 'What are you on about? Oh, I have needled you, which only proves my thesis: you like him, Cass, I can tell. *Lady Cassandra Gresham* – you'd be the wife of an earl.' He turned back to where Caraboo had been. 'Hell, the pigeon's flown. You don't think . . . ?' He pointed towards the parapet.

'No, you idiot! She went down while we were bickering.' Cassandra made her way back to the ladder.

'That wasn't bickering,' Fred said, following her. 'That was an insightful observation on my part. You and Edmund Gresham. It will happen.'

'Don't hold your breath,' Cassandra said. 'You know, I so look forward to your return from school, and then when you do come, I wish you away almost at once.'

As Professor Heyford set up his apparatus in the library, Caraboo watched through a crack in the door. Frederick Worrall was helping – she could hear them talking about electricity.

Mrs Worrall was excited: she was quoting passages from one of her books on the anthropology of primitive peoples of the southern hemisphere. Caraboo had looked at that very book only this morning. It was a favourite of hers – the pictures were wonderful, in full colour, so that it was like looking into another world.

Mrs Worrall stopped reading. 'You see, Fred,' she

said, 'the way she uses her knife, you haven't witnessed it, but Cassandra and I watched her use it on a pigeon – she calls pigeon *rampu* – the other day, and she knows what she is doing! It's awfully like the *kriss*, the knife used by the Malay. Stamford Raffles talks about it in his *History of Java*, see? And that's another of her words – *Javasu*, you see? Quite fascinating! You must read it – here, look . . .'

'Well, madam.' This voice, Caraboo reckoned, must be the professor. 'When your Caraboo has submitted to examination under electrical stimuli, you will at last be sure of the young lady's provenance.'

'What I expect he means, Mama, is that if you gave her a few volts she'd be talking in English in seconds.'

'Frederick!'

'You know what I think about the girl. And Papa agrees with me.'

'Your father has not yet made up his mind. He agrees she is not a beggar.'

'Hah!'

There was a buzzing sound from the library and the smell of singed horsehair.

Mrs Worrall gasped. 'My word, Professor, are you sure your apparatus is quite safe?'

In the hall, Caraboo studied herself in the large oval looking glass. The Princess wore a white muslin turban and the dress she had adapted herself, with a square neckline and cut short to the knee. She was barefoot, and the marble tiles of the hall were cool under her feet. She must remember that feeling. She must be icy today; she must not think of running out into the park, as far away as possible. Not quite yet.

Caraboo took a deep breath, then walked slowly into the library, as if entering a throne room, head held high, steps even and measured. She was a princess, she told herself, and as soon as these people, especially that smug Frederick Worrall, realized the fact, the better. It had been fun, seeing the look on Mr Frederick's face this morning; wiping that smile off his arrogant face would be worth any discomfort the professor might have in store for her.

'Good morning, Caraboo!' Mrs Worrall put down her book, opened her arms and embraced her.

Caraboo saluted, her right hand pressed flat against her left temple.

Mrs Worrall spoke slowly. 'This is Professor Heyford.'

The professor put out his hand, but Caraboo merely saluted, touching her right hand to her right temple.

'You see, Professor,' Mrs Worrall said. 'The little salute, see? Right for gentlemen, left for ladies. I have noted that she will not, or chooses not to, have any contact with the male. She will embrace me, she will allow

Cassandra to come close, but she will not shake hands with a man. Perhaps you have come across the like on your travels?'

'I am afraid the farthest my travels have taken me is Edinburgh.'

'Ah.' Mrs Worrall looked disappointed.

'However, I am an expert in theoretical linguistics and the utterly new sciences of phrenology and electronic deduction,' the professor said. 'I feel that we, at the heart of the British Empire, have no need to travel. The world has come to us. You see, Mrs Worrall, I believe that by the twenty-first century all other languages will decline into obsolescence. English will be paramount. It is a far superior language to any other. Indeed, my thesis is that other tongues are poor substitutes; merely half-baked gropings towards the proper and most ideal form of communication that is the English tongue.'

Mrs Worrall looked uneasy. 'But what of French? I imagined French to be sublime . . .'

Professor Heyford shook his head and flapped a hand. 'French is a mongrel tongue.' His tone was dismissive.

'As is English, surely,' she said confidently.

'Aha!' The professor jabbed a finger into the air. 'It may have begun so, but I can assure you, madam, that its pedigree is spotless! Spotless.'

Fred made a face. 'What exactly does that—?'

But Mrs Worrall cut him off. 'How does all this' – she waved a hand towards the apparatus – 'aid your study of linguistics and – what was it . . . ?'

'Phrenology – the deduction of character and disposition as manifested in the shape and formation of the head. All will be revealed!' The professor took a kind of shining brass skullcap out of a leather satchel.

Caraboo tried to keep her expression blankly calm.

Apparatus. Electricity. It meant nothing. The Princess Caraboo had no knowledge of these things. She had never, as a child, frequented Exeter Fair and seen the fairground booths which promised instant cure-alls by means of shocks and starts. Or the punters exiting those tents with their jelly legs and wild eyes.

Apparatus could mean anything. She would simply have to charm the professor the same way she had charmed everyone else.

Caraboo turned her smile up to dazzle.

'What exceptionally white teeth your Caraboo has,' the professor said, changing the subject. 'And so neat and even!'

He was studying her closely. *Good*, she thought.

'Teeth like that are signifiers of both honesty and openness. I must admit, she is a most interesting young woman.' He was turning the brass cap in his hands, and now Caraboo could see the wires that came out of it.

'It will be fascinating to see how she responds to the natural forces, and how they affect her speech.'

'And this will tell us where she is from?' Fred sounded unconvinced.

The professor was getting flustered. 'Let us begin, and all will be clear!'

Mrs Worrall squeezed Caraboo's hand reassuringly.

'Can you bring the girl over to the chair by the window, madam, and make her comfortable? Mr Worrall' – he looked at Fred – 'if you will make sure her wrists are firmly bound.' He passed Fred a couple of leather straps.

'Are you sure all this is quite necessary?' Fred could see that Caraboo was anxious, but the professor simply nodded.

Mrs Worrall made shushing sounds at her, as if she were a baby.

Fred leaned close and buckled up the straps. He smelled of sandalwood and citrus, clean and sharp, and not beer and tobacco, which was a comfort. Caraboo tried to imagine unicorns and leopards, but her breaths were quick and shallow.

'I think she is afraid,' Mrs Worrall said, looking worried herself. 'I am sure of it.'

'It will all be over in the blink of an eye!'

'And you are sure it is quite safe?'

'Utterly, madam.' The professor turned a handle on the wooden box, which he said was the generator. The buzzing sound Caraboo had heard earlier started up again. The professor unwound her turban, and she flinched and would have jumped up if she hadn't had been tied down. He smelled of mothballs and coal, and old soup. Her hair fell down and he tried to gather it up, making her break into a cold sweat. He touched her head, and – she couldn't help it – she screamed.

'Mrs Worrall! I would appreciate it if you could get your Miss Caraboo to be quiet!'

'I am trying!' Mrs Worrall smoothed the hair away from Caraboo's forehead. 'Fred, where is your sister? She has a way with Caraboo.'

'I cannot say, Mama. The last I heard, she was most keen to see the electrical demonstration.'

The professor put the metal cap on Caraboo's head and attached the wires. 'Mrs Worrall, please stand back.' He pulled a lever.

Caraboo shut her eyes as the hum intensified into an oppressive thrum. She steeled herself, gripping the arms of the chair so hard her knuckles showed white.

Whatever faced her now could not be worse than the things that had already befallen her. She repeated the words over and over in her head. All the bad things that had happened – the men in the woods, her dead

Solomon, the look on Robert Lloyd's face when she had seen him kissing another. She screwed her eyes shut. Those things had all happened to somebody else.

Caraboo prayed hard to her god.

'The poor child!'

'The power is surging!' the professor said.

Suddenly Caraboo felt the air being knocked clear out of her. She was reminded of a time in another life, when she was seven: a boy in the village had caught her under her ribs in a fight. She gasped for air. She could no more exclaim a word in English than she could in any other language. She had no breath at all.

There was a sizzling sound, and a loud *pop!* and again the smell of burning – though this time of human hair.

'Oh my!' Mrs Worrall said.

She began unbuckling Caraboo's straps and tore off the skullcap, then took a Turkish embroidered throw from the divan and flung it over Caraboo's head.

'Water! Quickly! Fred!'

Then Caraboo was aware of spreading damp – Fred, she supposed, had emptied the vase of flowers over her, and when the throw was removed she realized she was soaked through and had a lap full of flowers.

'There's something wrong with the conductors . . .' The professor was fussing over his apparatus.

'Are you all right, miss?' Fred said.

But Caraboo saw that he was looking at her chest under the wet dress, and she hated him for it.

Mrs Worrall hugged her, arms around her neck. 'Oh, you poor, dear girl.'

Caraboo was overcome with relief. She remembered her language and shouted at the professor, '*Justo no bo beek! No bo beek!*' She was shaking with cold and shock.

'She is still talking gibberish,' Fred said.

'The experiment is not over!' the professor told him. 'I have barely started. The subject has not recieved the required voltage!'

'I think the poor child has had more than enough of your volts, sir. Her hair is quite burned off!' Mrs Worrall said. 'And her demeanour proves she is not a fraud at all. Wouldn't a fraud have cried out in English? Professor, from now on, I will permit only the usual kind of enquiry – no more electricals!'

'But, madam—'

'Look at the poor girl! What have you done, sir?' Mrs Worrall brushed the burned strands of hair away.

'It is only hair, madam, no flesh wounds,' the professor insisted.

Caraboo flinched and scrabbled for her turban.

At that moment Cassandra burst in through the

French windows. Her cheeks showed a high colour and her eyes were shining.

'Oh! Did I miss the electricity?' She looked at Caraboo, drenched and burned. 'Oh no! What have you done to poor Caraboo?'

Cassandra ran across the room, and as she did so a single stalk of straw fell out of her hair and fluttered down to the carpet – *as if she had been in the stables, perhaps,* Caraboo thought, *flat on her back . . .*

5

A Man from the Sea

Knole Park House
Almondsbury
April 1819

Caraboo had risen early, as usual, to climb up to the roof, but then the rain started, so she took a handful of the pink flowers that grew up there and ran back inside. She paused at the foot of the ladder, not wanting to be shut away in her room, and made her way quietly towards the library.

The house was mostly still asleep. The servants were about – she glimpsed Pheobe at the end of a corridor lugging a bucket of coal for the early morning fires – but she did not expect to find Finiefs in the library—

He jumped up when she opened the door. He must have been sitting in the chair by the window, straining to read a book in the first glimmerings of light.

He glared at her, but Caraboo only smiled. 'I was
. . .' He stood up, the guilt had gone. 'I don't know
why I bother. Princess or not, you cannot understand me.'

Caraboo made for the globe and spun it so the world
rumbled around. Finiefs was making for the door, but
she reassured him in her language that she would not
tell a soul. She tucked the pink willow herb into his lapel
and saluted. For a moment she thought that Finiefs was
about to tell her off, but he simply bowed his head and
saluted her back.

Caraboo picked up the book he had been reading,
but she saw that it was in Greek.

'I think perhaps' – the steward saw her looking –
'that we both have our secrets. I would not want this
family to know the pattern of my life in Istanbul and
Alexandria. Maybe it is the same with you.' He smiled
at Caraboo for the first time – a kind, almost fatherly
smile – bowed once more and left.

Caraboo listened for his footsteps as they crossed the
marble hall and faded away. There was a tightness in
her throat, a catch of such pain that she could not hold
the tears back any longer. For a few minutes the Princess
was gone, and Mary Willcox hid herself behind the curtain and cried silently for all she had lost.

*

William Jenkins swept a huge cloud of dust out of the door of the inn. He had hardly slept last night. For a moment he leaned on his broom; he watched as the specks swirled in the sunlight, and thought of Miss Cassandra Worrall. In truth, he had thought of nothing else since yesterday. It had been like inhabiting a dream, a dream made real.

He closed his eyes and remembered, and he was there, in the stables at Knole Park.

'This way . . .' She had said it quietly, then put her hand out and took his, and led him into a storeroom. He followed, reminded of a picture in a book he had seen of some farmer's boy enchanted by a fairy queen. He was aware of the softness of her fingers, her palm; he put his hand up to her face, and she touched her lips against his fingertips, and he felt his heart beat so hard in his chest he thought it might burst.

'Miss Worrall—'

'Don't say anything, Will, please . . .' She was looking at him. Those blue eyes, dark and deep, bluer than the gentian flowers in the meadow.

He couldn't help himself. He kissed her.

For a second he thought she might scream, push him away, but she didn't. She held him close, kissed him back. He could taste her now – her mouth, her tongue. And the softness and heat of her body against him.

When they had broken apart she was smiling. And so they kissed again—

'Will! William?' his father shouted from inside the inn.

Will jumped clear out of his skin and began sweeping, fiercely.

'What are you up to?' Mr Jenkins said. 'You're sweeping so hard you'll have the stones off the ground. We need two barrels of ale and one of last year's cider fetched up from the cellar! Quick sharp, boy.'

Will sighed. He had come back from London for two reasons. The first was that Father had said he was poorly. Miraculously, as soon as Will returned, all ailments seemed to have vanished. Will was sure he had just wanted a cheap pair of hands.

The other reason he'd come home had been Cassandra. He had looked at her, wanted her for years, wondering if she would ever notice him.

Will smiled to himself and pushed the hair off his face. He had seen a miracle with his own eyes, felt that miracle kiss him. It had been worth leaving London and his new job ten times over for that.

'Will!' his father shouted again. 'I need those barrels before my beard grows long enough to wipe my arse. Stop mooning around, lad, and knuckle down. Is it some girl you've left in London making you so?' He snorted. 'When I was your age I was wed – that's the only cure for dreaming. You should settle down, and quick sharp.'

Will went down to the cellar; at least there he was out of sight. But his father was right about one thing. He wanted to be wed. The snag was, he couldn't see Miss Cassandra settling for a life in a country inn. Perhaps he should have stayed in London and tried to earn some money. Perhaps he would have to leave again and make his fortune before approaching her family; maybe old man Worrall would not let her go. He should definitely make his fortune before the family got wind of the romance. That would be hard – there were no streets paved with gold . . . but he would work himself to the bone for her, whatever it took.

He closed his eyes and remembered those kisses. Oh! It would be entirely worth it.

That afternoon the Gloucester-to-Bristol stage stopped at the Almondsbury smithy rather than in front of the inn, the lead horse having cast a shoe. A gentleman stepped down, stiff from travelling. Will, despatched to meet the coach, carried his trunk, which was old and battered and very heavy. The man was elderly and distinguished, white hair cut short, clothes well made but old – the cuffs of his sleeves were quite worn. Judging by his garments and his bearing, he'd had money once, Will thought, a good few years ago.

'This is Almondsbury?' The man spoke loudly, almost barking. 'How far to Knole Park?'

'Knole Park? The Worrall house?' Will asked. Perhaps he could see Cassandra sooner than he'd imagined.

'Aye, that's what I said, lad.'

'Yes, sir. Knole Park. On foot, a good three-quarter mile along this road, sir. But I could drive you, if you follow me to the Golden Bowl.'

'The inn?'

Will nodded.

'Right, good man. Yes. I'm Captain Palmer.' He put out his hand and Will shook it. 'Thirty years with the finest navy in the world. You serve rum?'

'Best Jamaican, sir, straight off the boat,' Will said, and for the first time the man's face softened.

When Will came in from readying the gig, Captain Palmer had worked his way through a third of a bottle of the Golden Bowl's best white rum. He was leaning on the counter telling tales of some kind of spirit to Mr Jenkins, who was listening, rapt.

'Imagine this . . .' The captain's eyes shone. 'The head of a woman – not just a woman – a girl, young and fresh. The most beautiful girl you've clapped eyes on: golden skin, black hair, eyes that'd melt a man with one look.'

Will saw his father nod, open-mouthed. 'What's she wearing, then? Some shift? Wet, mebbe?'

Will rolled his eyes. They were worse than school boys.

'Nothing! She's not wearing a stitch.' The captain leaned close. 'Not one scrap.'

'Ent she now?' Will was embarrassed to see that his father was almost drooling.

'No,' said the captain, pouring himself another measure. 'In fact, she don't even have a body, just her entrails and innards dangling down, glistening and pulsating as she floats through the air . . .'

Mr Jenkins pulled a face. 'That's not much of a bundle of fun.'

'Exactly! Exactly! The Penanggalan! Foulest fiend in all Malay – saw it with my own eyes, I did! On a moonlit night in old Jakarta, she floated past my window as clear as I see you. Blood dripped from her horrible mouth . . .'

'No!'

The captain lowered his voice. 'The thing turned, our eyes locked, just for a moment. I felt a chill in my heart as though it were gripped by ice.' He shook his head. 'I thought I was dead. I blinked, and in the instant my eyes were closed, she flew at me and I felt her mouth upon my neck, her foul breath hard against my face. See, here!'

Captain Palmer pulled his collar away from his neck. Will couldn't help looking, but he thought the marks might just be moles.

Mr Jenkins leaned closer. 'What happened then?'

'I felt the life draining out of me. My whole life flashed before my very eyes. The thing, the Penanggalan, was sucking out my vital force. With the last of my strength I fumbled in my pocket for my pistol. I was fading. I could feel the black veil of death falling . . . falling . . .'

Mr Jenkins gasped.

'I pulled the trigger. The thing fell to the floor in a juddering stinking black mess. And she screamed. The sound was the scream of Hell come to earth. I hope to God I never hear the like of it again . . .' The captain slammed the glass down onto the table. 'It's a miracle I lived to tell the tale.'

By the time Will got Captain Palmer and his trunk into the gig, there wasn't much he didn't know about Penanggalan or Pocong or any other Malay spirits and demons, and there wasn't much rum left either.

'You up to see the foreign girl, Captain? The one that speaks no English?' Will asked.

'That's why I'm here, lad – sent for to discover if she is indeed the genuine article.'

'They found her out on the Bristol road.'

'Did they now? They say she is most *interesting*.'

Will shrugged. 'She is passing pretty – good teeth – though I seen darker-skinned girls two a penny in London.'

'Two a penny, you say?'

Will flushed. 'Not like that, sir, no . . .'

The old man laughed.

'There's a professor come up from London at Knole Park, trying to talk to her.'

'What's the fellow's name?'

'Heyford, Professor Heyford.'

Captain Palmer harrumphed. 'Can't say I know the name.'

'He works with electricity, I heard.'

The captain smiled. 'Well, I hope the fellow knows what he is doing. I speak eight varieties of dialect, don't you know. Lived out East for years – best time of my life, young man.' He looked at Will. 'You should travel, son, get yourself out of here and see the world.' He leaned back and belched. 'Make your fortune.'

Will smiled. 'I need a fortune, sir,' he said as he urged the horse on, 'and no mistake.'

'Then you'd better be on that boat quick sharp! They say the days of the Sugar Barons are over. The nigrahs will be turning on us afore long, after what was done to them.' Captain Palmer shook his head. 'America has furs, though, and silver – lots of space for a young man.'

'It is a long way, sir.'

The captain waved a hand in the air. 'Mark my words, nothing's a long way any more. These days a man can be across the Atlantic in a matter of weeks. Why, the world shrinks so fast I wager a man'll stride around the globe in days by the time you reach my age.'

'I worked in an inn in London, sir,' Will said, 'and there were folk back off the boats saying just that.' He drove the cart through the gates of Knole Park. 'But you have me thinking, sir. I do need to make my fortune, and quick . . . Oh, I'll work hard, there's none can match me when I put my mind to it. Then I can come back and, well, I don't like to say anything more, sir, but I need to come back a gentleman.' He sighed as he looked at the house at the end of the drive. It was as least four, maybe five, times as big as the Golden Bowl. He needed to show Cassandra Worrall that he was serious. That he could keep her, and provide for her – he let out a long sigh – in the manner to which she was accustomed.

America! Will saw himself in a few years, wearing one of them fancy coats with a plush beaver collar those colonialists wore, over a finer suit than Cassandra's beau nasty of a brother could ever afford. Then he would get down from his horse and stride up to old Mr Worrall and ask outright for his daughter's hand – and, what's more, get it gladly.

Will pulled gently on the reins and the horse came to a halt. 'Sir, Captain Palmer, we're here.'

There was a snort from the captain, and Will realized that he was fast asleep.

Caraboo saw the gig turn into the drive from her hiding place in the branches of the large beech tree that grew at the front of Knole Park.

She was hiding from Professor Heyford, who had insisted on yet another cranial exploration. He had carried out two already, and as far as Caraboo could fathom it was an excuse to stand exceptionally close and run his hands all over her head while making various pronouncements. It was close to torture.

During the last two, Professor Heyford had deduced that Caraboo was from the Orient and that she liked dancing. He divined that she was young and vigorous and her teeth were proof of good family; according to the professor she was definitely of noble birth. Truly the man had as much insight as a card table!

But at least Caraboo had given him no reason to think her a fraud, and he had neither the wit nor the knowledge to see past the end of his own nose. Or perhaps, she thought, he wanted only to impress his patron, Mrs Worrall, by going along with her own impressions. People, she thought to herself, did so want to believe a good tale.

Lies were easy; it was always the truth that was difficult.

Caraboo was sure of one thing: she had nothing to fear from the professor. Mrs Worrall was beginning to find him tiresome and was looking forward to the arrival of Captain Palmer, a navy man and explorer who spoke, apparently, ten languages. Perhaps, Caraboo thought, this was him coming now.

As the gig came closer she recognized the driver: it was William Jenkins from the inn, the boy Cassandra wouldn't stop talking about. In the seat next to him was an elderly, white-haired gentleman, hat off, mouth open, fast asleep.

William was good looking – Caraboo could see why Cassandra had fallen for him, and he had seemed a nice enough young man. He wasn't like Frederick Worrall, talking to a girl while he stared at her breasts or her legs. He was decent, she was sure, but she also knew that an affair like theirs could never end well. Caraboo sighed. The Princess would never fall in love.

She watched as Will shook the man awake and took his trunk down off the cart. It looked heavy; Caraboo hoped he didn't have anything to do with electricity locked up inside. She dismissed the idea – this man looked too old to be swept up by modern fads and fancies. He walked with a strange gait – a man who had obviously spent a lot of time at sea. This was the 'second opinion' which had caused

Professor Heyford to go into a sulk.

The captain was a drinker, his red nose made that clear, and the way he talked – not just with his voice, which Caraboo could hear from her hiding place, but with his arms, with his body – made him seem twice as tall as he really was.

'So, farewell, lad,' he roared. 'Send me a letter from Philadelphia!' He saluted Will as the front door opened. Caraboo frowned – was Will off to America?

'That lad's a diamond and no mistake!' he said as he clicked his heels and bowed to Finiefs and Mrs Worrall. 'Captain Palmer, late of Sumatra, at your service. Pleased to make your aquaintance, I'm sure.'

Up in the tree Caraboo smiled. Perhaps this sea captain would have more luck with her. After all, if he could see that William Jenkins was a diamond, then he was bound to discover that Caraboo was a princess.

She waited until Will had led the horse and cart round to the stables, then jumped softly down to the ground and ran round the side of the house. Even though she knew that Cassandra's love affair with Will was doomed, she wanted to see her friend happy, as she would be once she discovered that her love was here at Knole.

Cassandra was in the schoolroom with Miss Marchbanks, and Caraboo decided to make an entrance.

She climbed onto the balcony of the room next door and jumped in through the window, making the governess start.

'Oh my word!' Miss Marchbanks clutched her chest. 'It is that girl again! Can you not get Mrs Worrall to keep her *out* of the schoolroom when we are working!'

Caraboo saluted her, pressing her left hand to her forehead and biting her lip to prevent herself laughing. Then she tugged Cassandra's hand. '*Ake, Cass-andra! Ake!*'

'I think she wants me to go with her, Miss Marchbanks. *Ake* means "come".' Cassandra was already getting up.

'Well, I suppose you might learn a new language yet,' the governess sighed. 'But it's hardly French, is it?'

Caraboo pulled Cassandra down the stairs, into the garden and then through to the stable yard.

'Caraboo, what are you doing?'

She made as if she wanted to lead her past the stables to the lake, but Cassandra stopped dead and squeezed her hand as she recognized the gig from the Golden Bowl, standing there in the stable yard.

Mr Vaughan, the coachman, was talking to William Jenkins – something about the Golden Bowl's horse, which looked as if it had seen better days.

Caraboo felt Cassandra take a deep breath. She let go of her hand and stepped back so that Cassandra wouldn't see the wry smile that crossed her face.

'Ah, Vaughan!' Cassandra said. 'Is Zephyr quite well? Only I looked over his saddle and there seemed to be some stitching that was irritating his back. I wonder, could you take a look?' She smiled, and Caraboo thought that she sounded completely natural. She had obviously lied before, and often.

'Certainly, Miss Worrall.'

Cassandra leaned close. 'Now there's only Stephen to get rid of,' she said, looking at the stable boy, who was cleaning out a loose box across the yard.

Out of the corner of her eye Caraboo saw her lead William Jenkins into the grain store. Even if her heart did get broken, Cassandra had so many people around her who loved her; people who would help her. In any case, Caraboo told herself, a girl like Cassandra would never need help. It was Will, she thought, who would be hurt. Mary Willcox, far away in Exeter and London, knew that love was poisonous, that men would only hurt you, but perhaps the Princess thought differently.

Will reappeared a few minutes later, climbed into the gig and drove off towards Almondsbury. When the coast was clear, Cassandra emerged. 'I am meeting him after church this Sunday, in the field beyond the grave-yard . . .' She smoothed her hair down before linking her arm through Caraboo's. 'Oh, Caraboo. I wish you could understand me! William is such a gentleman, and so handsome! And his kisses! There is none in the whole county – not even Edmund – that could hold a candle to him.'

Caraboo said nothing. Cassandra took her by the hand and led her away from the house. 'His eyes are, I swear, the bluest I have seen!' She lowered her voice, even though there was no one within earshot. 'You should have heard him, Caraboo – the way he spoke to me, touched me! I swear my heart nearly burst with the thrill of it.' Cassandra shuddered, remembering. 'He has sworn his love to me, said he had thought of me every day he was away in London. He sees a future for us, together!'

Caraboo thought hard. She should open her mouth there and then and, in the plainest English, spell out that there was no future in it. That if William Jenkins was not lying – and she thought it unlikely that he was – then Cassandra was lying to herself. She was not the sort of girl who would enjoy the life of an innkeeper's wife.

Caraboo recognized the look in Cassandra's eyes. In many ways, she thought, there was little to choose between love and madness.

'And the smell of his skin!' Cassandra was almost swooning. 'I would be lost to kissing—' She stopped dead.

She had looked up to see Fred come swaggering across the yard. Caraboo thought she would like to take a stick and hit him hard across the back of his knees, so that he fell face down in the slurry Stephen had just swept out of the stable. She pictured his pristine cream trousers – the latest fashion – covered with dung, and smiled.

'I have been looking for you two everywhere. Captain Palmer is waiting in the drawing room and he absolutely can't wait to meet our foreign friend.'

'Fred, her name is Princess Caraboo.'

'Yes, and I am Napoleon Bonaparte, Emperor of all the World!'

The three of them entered the drawing room, where Mrs Worrall and the professor were already seated, while Captain Palmer stalked up and down, cutting the air with a knife. It had a serpentine blade, like a child's drawing of a wave, and a bright red silken tassel on the handle. Caraboo had seen one exactly like it in Mrs Worrall's books.

The captain had the whole party so enthralled by his tale that no one could take their eyes off him – although Professor Heyford's expression was more than a little sour, his finger tapping irritably at his leg as the captain spoke. It had been some time since he had last been invited to demonstrate any of his equipment.

'. . . So you see, the tiger almost had the better of our party—' He stopped abruptly when he saw Caraboo, and she saluted him, right hand to temple.

He looked her up and down, and then saluted her back.

'*Manjitoo, Lazor.*' Caraboo went on to salute the professor and Mrs Worrall. Then her eyes fixed upon the captain's knife, at which he solemnly handed it over. She took it, feeling the weight of it in her hands, then making slashing motions, once, twice, a third time – perilously close to the cheek of Frederick Worrall, causing him to step back.

Caraboo studied the knife closely. It was beautiful, and so shiny she could see her own face in it. She remembered what it had said in Mrs Worrall's book, and traced her finger along the blade so that it drew blood. She heard Mrs Worrall gasp. Then she took the blade over to the window, where Mrs Worrall kept a large pot plant. Caraboo took a leaf and wiped it over the blade, and Captain Palmer almost shouted with excitement.

'There! There! Did you see that!' He pointed at the knife and the plant. 'See! It proves that the girl is most definitely a Malay, from one of the islands. They use poison like that! Just like that! Wipe it over the knife – kills the damned monkeys in double-quick time!'

'Well I never!' Mrs Worrall said.

Caraboo noticed that Frederick Worrall said nothing; he merely re-crossed his legs the other way.

'*Kriss!*' Captain Palmer said, pointing at the knife.

'*Kriss*,' Caraboo said back and nodded. '*Kriss beek*.'

'By Jove, that's it! She think's it's good.'

'Yes! Yes, she does,' Cassandra said, nodding. 'That's her word for good – *beek*!'

The captain smiled. 'Didn't I say there isn't a language in those islands I don't know a little of?'

Everyone was grinning and nodding and smiling – except Professor Heyford, who looked piqued, and Fred, who looked indifferent.

'*Javasu?*' Caraboo said, looking straight at the captain. He was as big a liar as she was, wasn't he?

'*Jav-a-su?*' he said back slowly, nodding.

Captain Palmer indicated that she should sit, then began to babble at her in what sounded like a variety of different languages. Caraboo kept her eyes on him at all times, and in some of the gaps she talked back.

Mrs Worrall and Cassandra watched, rapt.

The captain had a book in his hand, and Caraboo saw that it was the same as Mrs Worrall's, about the islands of the East Indian Ocean, Batavia and Malaya.

He flipped the pages, and pointed to a picture of some fruit.

'*Ananas!*' Caraboo exclaimed.

'My, my,' Mrs Worrall said, 'isn't that French for pineapple?'

'It's Eastern originally,' Captain Palmer said seriously, turning round in his chair to face her. 'Proves again – and without a doubt, I might say – that what we're dealing with here is a Malay.'

He skipped on a few pages, and there was an illustration of the temple at Borobudur in Java. Then on a few pages more to one of peacock feathers. Caraboo stopped him, and indicated that back home they adorned her turban. She knew from Mrs Worrall's library that peacock feathers were a sign of royalty; surely Captain Palmer knew this too.

'Ah!' he said. 'The maid's from one of the islands. There's no doubt. And the peacock feathers: a sure sign of nobility. Now, if you would, madam, fetch me a small tot of rum and a globe – perhaps we can discover the true and most likely origins of your house guest!' He turned and spoke in his strange language to Caraboo, who smiled, and babbled back.

'What do you think she is saying, Mama?' Cassandra said.

Fred leaned back in his chair. 'Gobbledygook – I'd put money on it.'

'Shh, Fred,' Mrs Worrall said. 'Captain Palmer is a hero, and a gentleman. Even your father is aware of Captain Palmer's exploits in the East Indies!'

The globe was brought in and Captain Palmer pointed at Java, talking to Caraboo all the while. She nodded, and traced a long looping path with her finger across the seas, under the tip of Africa and up the coast as far as France. She kept her face utterly straight. She and Captain Palmer were both talking nonsense. She knew that. He *must* know that. Or perhaps, Caraboo thought, she was indeed real. Perhaps it only took someone else to see that. She felt giddy. Perhaps it was Mary Willcox who was a figment of Caraboo's imagination. Perhaps this was reality and the previous seventeen years had been a mixture of dreams and nightmares.

Captain Palmer poured himself a second glass of rum and addressed the company. 'Well, our young Caraboo here has quite a tale to tell.'

The Princess sat up straight. She wondered what she was meant to have told him. She stroked her leopard, which had, in her mind's eye, wound itself around her legs.

'I knew it!' Mrs Worrall clapped her hands.

'Now, I don't pretend to know all the ins and outs

of her dialect, but from what I can understand we have here among us a very special lady who has endured a most terrible and dangerous journey . . .'

'I never doubted it! Frederick, your father will have to believe me now,' Mrs Worrall said.

'As I intimated earlier, Caraboo is no common or garden Malay, oh no.'

The eyes of the whole company were fixed on Captain Palmer.

'I believe young Caraboo is a noblewoman from Javasu, captured by pirates in the South China Seas and cruelly torn from her home, from all she knows . . .'

Caraboo wanted to nod, but held back and concentrated on the knife, feeling the silky tassle and watching it flash in the light.

'A noblewoman?' Mrs Worrall said. 'Like a countess?'

'Yes, yes,' Captain Palmer replied, 'or maybe a—'

'Perhaps a princess?' Cassandra gasped.

'Exactly right, young lady. This young woman, I have no doubt at all, is indeed a princess.'

'A princess!' Fred said it dismissively, but Caraboo could hear the doubt in his voice. 'You're quite sure? I mean to say—'

Captain Palmer swivelled to face Frederick Worrall. 'Young man, I have been around the world and back again. I have seen more of the wonders that it has to offer in my three score years than most men see in a lifetime. I have met royalty from the Guinea coast to Coromandel and all the way to China. Believe me, I know a princess when I find one.' He pointed at Caraboo. 'And here she is!'

Caraboo looked meekly around the company. She did not blush because she had to pretend that she could not understand a word, but the story about the pirates was an embroidery by Captain Palmer so audacious that she could not believe the Worralls weren't throwing the pair of them out and calling the magistrates. Is that really what he had heard when she had spoken to him? She had to work hard not to smile.

Even if she *had* understood, the fact that she was indeed a princess was something she had known all along, so it was hardly a shock or a revelation. But now the whole household, not least Mr Frederick Worrall, was aware of the fact too.

6

IN THE COURT OF CARABOO

Knole Park House
May 1819

'I don't know how much I believe you, you know.' Frederick Worrall had been watching her. He had climbed up onto the roof and was leaning against the tiles in his dressing gown. His chest was bare and his skin was the palest gold in the dawn light.

Princess Caraboo's hand went to her kriss. Another week had run past like water and she was still here. It was her own fault. She moved away. It was his roof, after all. His roof, his house, his life.

The clock on the stable block said six; the air was early morning sparkling.

'No salute?' Fred said. 'Don't I even deserve that?'

Caraboo said nothing – he was mocking her. If he came any closer . . .

He put his hands up. 'I'm not here for you! You don't think—?' He looked faintly disgusted. 'Look, Caraboo, Princess of wherever, my intentions are honourable. I just came up here because I couldn't sleep, that's all. Came up for some air.' He looked around, surveying the park and the country beyond. 'This is a grand place up here. No idea why I never bothered before.' He took a deep breath, drinking in the air. 'You can see so far . . .'

Caraboo remained wary. After all, she could understand only a few of his words.

Fred turned round. 'I still don't know what game you're playing, but I'll swear you're playing at something – even if that jabber you and the captain spout is a proper language, even if you are a bona fide princess . . . But you know, so long as you don't hurt my family, I'm not sure I can be bothered to care . . .' He looked off into the distance, his arms behind his head, and said nothing more.

Caraboo got up and began to walk back towards the trapdoor. This boy would not know trouble if it jumped up and hit him over the head.

'Caraboo,' he called. 'Princess Caraboo.'

She stopped.

'Sorry.' He said it again, more slowly: 'Sorry.'

She had never heard Fred Worrall apologize before.

Perhaps she had acheieved a little victory. She went back to her altar and sat down.

'You know what, Caraboo?' Fred said. 'Perhaps you could help me. Yes, I think you could – after all, you have no idea what I'm saying.'

He looked lost, and Caraboo found herself wondering why. What could trouble a young man like this, with every advantage? He had money, he was strong and healthy; surely he had never had to be anybody but himself.

She turned round.

'I could tell you all the family secrets,' he was saying, 'and you'd just nod and smile.'

Caraboo said nothing; just stared into the distance beyond the park. Even though she would have enjoyed pushing him head first off the roof, she had to admit she wanted to hear what he had to say.

'I don't know quite what's wrong with me,' Fred sighed.

Caraboo kept her face blank. *Where shall I start?* she could have said. *The list is very long.* Instead she had to bite her tongue.

Fred Worrall reminded her of a prize bull, groomed to golden perfection for a country show – and, oh, how he knew it. She resolved not to give him even a sideways glance.

'I thought . . .' he said. 'I thought I knew everything about women, about girls.'

I bet you did.

He said nothing for a long while. And Caraboo was about to get up and take the strawberries she'd collected and go inside, when he sighed again. A long desperate sigh that sounded as if it came from the heart. She looked at him for a second. *He has no heart*, she reminded herself.

'Someone said something to me. It was nothing, really; she was nothing.'

Princess Caraboo felt the anger rising up. She swallowed, calmed herself. 'No-thing?' she said, as if it was the first time she had ever said the word.

He smiled. 'No, not nothing. She was a tart.'

What did she expect from someone like him?

'A tart. And I can't stop thinking about it. She said that nobody would ever love me, and I know it's ridiculous, but it felt like a curse.'

Caraboo cocked her head as if she knew nothing. Inside, Mary Willcox smiled.

'Then I thought – How will I know if anyone loves me, if all I have ever known is a love I have bought?' He laughed. 'Even saying that aloud is ridiculous, isn't it? I mean love! But what if those looks and sighs are all pretend? How will I ever know when I am really loved?'

He made a face, turned away. 'I'm an idiot.'

Yes. Yes, you are. Caraboo popped a strawberry into her mouth and watched a trio of swallows trace a series of perfect arcs in the sky. She lay back on the tiles, and thought, *How do any of us know?* She remembered Robert Lloyd, Solomon's father, laughing at her. He had promised her so much, professed love all the while, and she had believed him, never once guessing that it wasn't so; never imagining that her Robert could return to London married to another. Even when she saw the proof. She was nothing to him. No-thing.

How could anyone know if love was true or false?

'I am an idiot,' Fred said again, sitting up.

'Id-i-ot?' Caraboo said aloud. *How right you are, sir.*

He shook his head and smiled. 'Forget it. I think love is for air-headed girls like my sister, who swoon over young men.' He gestured dismissively. 'That's all.'

Caraboo looked at him. She was enjoying this. 'Love?' she said. He was vulnerable after all. Somewhere under all that bluster and bragging he was afraid. *Good*, she thought.

Fred Worrall pushed his hair out of his eyes and looked at her. Caraboo reminded herself that you could not trust surface appearances at all.

'Love . . .' He put his hand upon his chest and she mirrored the action.

Perhaps she could hurt him the way she'd been hurt; the way he had, no doubt, hurt others. Perhaps Caraboo had a purpose here after all. Fred was not just a young man, he was the very worst of every young man on this earth. From Solomon's father, who reckoned himself the Romeo of Clerkenwell, to those animals on the road . . .

Her eyes met Fred's for a fraction of a second, then he coughed and turned away. 'I have been thinking too much. So help me, there's nothing else to do out here!' He laughed to himself. 'You are too damnably pretty to be real, do you know that?' he told her.

Yes, she thought, *I could make you sorry*. She smiled at him. Just a little.

'I bet you know that,' he went on. 'Most girls know how they look, how they stand. I've seen it in Cassandra: she turns her face in order that Edmund can see the light fall on her cheek just so. Girls can't pass any mirror – any shiny cousin of a mirror – without a good look at themselves. To make sure their outward appearance is appealing, even when their hearts . . .' He waved a hand. 'Girls are all liars.'

Caraboo reminded herself that she did not understand. 'Li-ars?' she asked.

'Cheats. They feign love, whether for money or marriage—'

'Caraboo no cheat!' She was so indignant that Fred couldn't help smiling.

'No. Maybe Caraboo no cheat . . . but she'd be the only woman in the world who wasn't!' He shook his head and laughed, and she couldn't be cross with him because he was right. Caraboo didn't cheat and she didn't lie – because she didn't exist.

Anyway, she wanted to say that it wasn't just girls, it was everyone. Everybody told lies – to each other, to themselves – all the time: lies soften the blows of life, everyone knew that. Perhaps Frederick Worrall was an even bigger fool than he looked. This could be – *would* be – easy.

Caraboo took a handful of tiny wild strawberries from her altar and put one down near his feet.

Fred reached forward and picked one up. 'Thank you,' he said. He smelled of clean linen and something deeper, something musky. *It might even be enjoyable*, Caraboo thought, and moved closer.

He gazed into her eyes for a little too long, and Caraboo looked away. She was a princess, after all; she would make him work hard. She would make him regret that he had ever set eyes on her; she would break his gilt-edged, feather-bedded heart.

A formation of geese honked overhead, heading west, and Caraboo followed them with her eyes. She would head home too, she thought. Home? Her own life, her real life, was poor and mean and sad compared to Caraboo's. Father wouldn't be pleased to see her, not really. She shut her eyes. Where else on earth could she go? Who wanted or cared for Mary Willcox of Devon?

Princess Caraboo sat up and blinked Mary Willcox away. Fred Worrall was beautiful – like a painting or a sculpture brought to life. She smiled, showing her very good teeth, divided up the remaining strawberries into two piles and pushed one towards him.

This is not real, only a story come to life.

'You shouldn't be kind to me, Princess.' Fred sighed and pushed his hair away from his face. 'I know I do not deserve it.'

No, she would have liked to say, *you do not.*

'I have done too many reprehensible things. Selfish things.' He shook his head. 'I have been mean about you as well, though I don't expect you've noticed.'

He was so short-sighted!

'But you know,' he said, 'I have never made a friend of a girl. Never. Not even once.' He ate a strawberry and the juice ran down his chin. 'I think you would make a most excellent friend.'

Caraboo cocked her head. If he knew who she really

was, he would never speak to her again. Even less want to listen to her.

But he was never going to know. He was going to love her. She bit into a strawberry as artlessly as she could. He would no doubt think it natural for her to smile so. Caraboo lay back on the tiles. How long to break a man's heart? She didn't know. She knew hers had snapped in two in moments. She had found Robert in the arms of Jenny Pierce the day after she'd told him she was pregnant. Up until that second she had been planning their wedding – a small one, admittedly – well, the cheaper the better, with a baby on the way. But he would be hers. She had loved him and he had thrown her affection away like so much dust.

She blinked. That was a different life.

Princess Caraboo looked at Fred. Could she do it in a week? It would be far too dangerous to stay any longer. Yes, she said to herself, another week and then Caraboo would vanish, never to be seen again, and Mr Frederick Worrall's world would come crashing down around his ears. One man to suffer in the place of all men.

Their hands touched over the strawberries and Princess Caraboo looked away. Out of the corner of her eye she saw him smile.

Perhaps it would take less than one week . . .

Suddenly Cassandra, still in her nightgown, burst

through the trapdoor. 'There you both are! I almost had Bridgenorth send out a search party!'

'I am quite safe,' Fred said. 'We've had breakfast.'

Cassandra sat down next to her brother and leaned against his shoulder. They were both so expensive looking, Caraboo thought; fair and gold and perfect.

She stood up.

'No, Caraboo! Stay. It's so lovely up here!' Cassandra took the last strawberry. 'And, Fred, you never want to be with me, to talk to me, any more. All you do is tease.'

'That is not true!' Fred said, hurt. 'You're always busy. Either Miss Marchbanks has you tied to a chair in the schoolroom or you're off on that pony of yours.'

'He is not a pony, he's a horse. And I might be busy . . .' she said.

Fred looked at her, one eyebrow raised. 'I would swear you are up to something, little sister.'

'I'm not up to anything,' she said. 'But you . . . is something the matter, Fred?'

'Hmm?'

'Have you a girl in London sweet on you?'

Caraboo saw Fred look away.

'Of course. They fall at my feet in the streets,' he said coolly.

Cassandra looked serious. 'Have you ever been in

love?' she asked. '*Really* in love? Has there ever been anyone you would wish to marry?'

'My God, Cassandra, have you been talking to Mama? I am not marrying. I am grown cynical already. Girls are all liars and marriage is flatty catching by another name.'

Cassandra hit him playfully. 'You are no fun at all. Diana Edgecombe is sweet on you.'

'I did rather know that, yes.'

'So why don't you marry her? She is fair, and a good match.'

He rolled his eyes. 'I am eighteen.' He looked at his sister. 'I say! It's you, isn't it? That's where all this talk of love comes from. It's *you*! So Edmund will have to fight for you, then?'

Cassandra blushed to match the strawberries.

'I'm right! I am! Who is it, Cass? I will *make* you tell me!'

She dashed over to the trapdoor and down the ladder, with Fred hard on her heels.

Caraboo was left on her own. She would do it, she thought. He would love someone who did not even exist.

She turned her face towards the sun. Caraboo could do it – after all, she was a princess, the world bent to her will. And Caraboo was a wonderful invention; everyone loved her. It would make a fine and most worthwhile diversion.

She looked down over the estate and began to plan Caraboo's first move. Of course, it would look as though she gave not one fig for him. She would hunt and swim and climb. She would not simper or play the doxy, like every other girl he'd known. She would play the Tom Rig all the while, and reel him in.

Men, all men, were simple, stupid things to Princess Caraboo.

She skipped down the steps, two at a time, picturing, in her mind's eye, Frederick Worrall reduced to tears and eaten up with despair. She would head straight for the island, and would lay a decent bet, had she any coin, on him arriving before lunch time, looking for her.

Caraboo changed into what she called her hunting dress – a confection she had made with the help of Cassandra, knee-length, light brown Indian cotton. She tied a belt around her waist and tucked her knife in, and ran towards the open doors that led to the park.

She saw Mrs Worrall, the professor and Captain Palmer deep in discussion in the library, and even though Mrs Worrall beckoned her over, Caraboo smiled and shouted back that she was off to the island. Of course, they didn't understand her.

'What was that?' Mrs Worrall asked the captain.

He answered something about prayer, which Caraboo thought was foolish given that the household knew she prayed on the roof. But it was, she had to agree, a safe bet. The captain had saluted, though, so she had no choice but to stop. For the first time she felt annoyed with him, whereas before she had only felt grateful. She saluted back. '*Manjitoo*' – to the captain – '*Manjitoo*' – the professor – '*Lazor*' – to Mrs Worrall.

'*Ana*,' she said, pointing outside.

'Oh, I know that one: *ana*, wa-ter!' Mrs Worrall smiled.

'Wa-ter, yes.' Caraboo nodded.

'Oh, she will soon be fluent in English, I have no doubt, Captain Palmer.'

'No doubt,' he agreed.

'Oh, Princess, we are making such plans!' Mrs Worrall beamed. 'And, Captain, could you ask Caraboo if we could possibly have some samples of her hand-writing to send to Edinburgh and Oxford?'

Captain Palmer frowned, and Caraboo thought he looked for a moment like he might be about to argue – but Professor Heyford cut in, 'A most excellent idea, I am personally acquainted with several of the finest graphologists in the country . . .'

Mrs Worrall clapped her hands. 'How wonderfully fortunate, don't you think, Captain?'

Captain Palmer shot Heyford a look sharp as knives, but he nodded politely at Mrs Worrall and babbled a suitably Javanese request. Caraboo nodded regally. There could be no harm in it. She would be long gone by the time any professors had deigned to reply. And if they were like Heyford, she thought, there was a good chance she could fool them too.

'The whole county is so interested in you – not to mention the Bath Institute and the newspapers . . . I was thinking of a party, to introduce you to society.'

Caraboo smiled placidly at her hostess, then saluted again and made to leave. The captain shouted after her – some senseless babble. She turned and nodded, and saw that he was staring after her in a most unpleasant fashion. Probably the result of too much rum and his unconscionably early start, she thought, and finally escaped out into the sun.

The island was perfect. Princess Caraboo knew that wherever she had come from, this small island was her true home, her Javasu. She lit a fire – no doubt the smoke would work in much the same way as a royal standard flying from the tower of a palace: the Princess is in residence. She sat down and laid her hunting dress out on some branches to dry. There was no point in starting to hunt before Fred arrived. So after she had retrieved the bow she had left on her last visit and made a few more arrows, she cleared a space on the ground and began to practise her handwriting in order that dear Mrs Worrall should not be disappointed. Using a twig, she traced curls and arabesques like she'd seen in another of Mrs Worrall's books.

'Bravo, Princess, Bravo!' Fred was here already. He had been watching her.

Princess Caraboo shinned up the nearest tree, grabbing her hunting gown as she went. She yelled the best Javasu insults she could think of; then, once she was sitting fully clothed in the crook of the small chestnut tree, she realized that she could not have played it better if she had tried.

Except that her kriss was down by the fire.

'Are you after this, Princess?' Fred passed it up. 'Look, I mean no harm.' He raised his hands. 'No harm,' he repeated, more slowly.

But Caraboo wasn't ready to forgive him yet.

'I'm sorry, but you looked so . . . You were writing, weren't you?' He had managed to stamp all over it, but she nodded.

'Mama will be fascinated,' he said.

That's the idea, she said to herself, and took a deep breath. She reminded herself that she was supposed to be beguiling this self-important beau. She shinned back down the tree, saluted and bowed, and he bowed a clumsy reponse, his blond hair flopping over his face. 'Sor-ry,' he said. 'Fred – is – sor-ry.'

Two apologies in one day. She wanted to smile.

'Caraboo hunt,' she said, picking up her bow and arrows, and darted into the trees ahead of him. She was small and nimble, but he struggled to keep up with her. It was like having a stupid, clumsy older brother, Caraboo thought. Twice she lost a pigeon because of an 'I say' or a 'Wouldn't fishing be simpler, Princess?'

But he did call her 'Princess', and when she brought down the first bird he seemed genuinely impressed.

'Good shot, Princess. I never thought those arrows could do any damage at all.'

She gave him her best withering look as she picked up the pigeon and removed the arrow, its sharpened tip red with blood.

He looked away first. Princess Caraboo was enjoying herself.

She tracked another bird, and made him crouch down close beside her, her finger to her lips for quiet, a good deal of her skin pressed against his fashionably tight, pale breeches. She passed him the bow and arrow and told him, with actions, that he should shoot. Caraboo was looking forward to seeing him fail.

Fred took the hand-made bow and took aim. He hit

the bird cleanly and lethally with his first shot, and she had to hide her disappointment.

'I hit it!' His smile lit up his face. 'Wait till I tell Ed about this – doesn't half knock potting ducks into a cocked hat and no mistake.'

Caraboo stood, clapping her hands and saluting him. She spoke to him in her language, telling him that he was an excellent shot, and also a prime strutting cockscomb.

He bowed and said, 'Princess, whoever you are, you are a marvel. Shall we take these back to the house?'

Caraboo simply picked up the pigeon and walked back to where the little fire had almost burned itself out. With gestures and signs she directed him to pluck the birds while she built up the fire.

'Plucking! Surely *you* should deal with the birds, and *I* the fire? Isn't that a more natural division of labour?'

Caraboo made a face that said she didn't understand. With mime and action she directed him to the birds again and strode off. She heard him curse but didn't turn round.

'As the Princess wishes . . .' He was mocking her, but she took no notice.

When she returned with an armful of twigs, Fred was sitting on a fallen tree with a still mostly feathered bird in his lap.

'This is interminable!' he said, looking at her.

She fed the fire, took the other bird and had its feathers off and its guts out in seconds. She spatchcocked it on a grid of twigs, propped it up over the flames, and coolly passed Fred the knife.

She didn't help. She sat back, leaning against a tree, arms folded, as her pigeon began to roast. She half shut her eyes, enjoying the spectacle of Frederick Worrall trying and failing. He had obviously never gutted anything in all his eighteen years. Suddenly he swore loudly and she saw that he had cut himself.

Princess Caraboo grinned at the sight of Fred, his breeches covered in blood and mud and grass stains, laid low by a dead pigeon. He looked thunderously at her, brushed the hair out of his eyes, only managing to smear yet more blood across his face. He looked like one of the noble savages in his mother's books, she thought. She told him this, in her made-up language, but he only scowled, prompting her to laugh.

'Just because I cannot prepare a pigeon for the table!' He threw down the sad, mangled little ball of feathers and flesh that had once been a bird.

Princess Caraboo scolded him. *That was food*, she said through mime.

He sighed. 'I will go back to the house – I won't eat your luncheon, Princess.'

He stood up to leave, but Caraboo reached for his arm and pulled him back towards the fire. It was, she thought, the first time she had touched a man for a very long while. This was lost on Fred, but he did sit down again.

'You are sure you want me at your table, Princess? I would make a very poor member of your tribe, would I not?'

'Tribe?' she said, head on one side.

'Tribe. Clan? Family? Fam-i-ly?' Fred pointed at himself. 'Cassandra, sister, Mrs Worrall, mother, Mr Worrall, father.' He sighed. 'I'd rather be in your tribe than mine, to be honest.'

Caraboo took up the mangled bird and started to pluck and clean it.

'All this living in the woods, hunting and swimming, sleeping under the stars – but I don't even know if you do that, do you? Perhaps you have some kind of native huts . . . I slept out once when I was young – never told a soul. Heavens, Ed would think I was on the road to Bedlam if I told him about this . . .'

Caraboo was making a grid to hold Fred's pigeon.

'But at least there'd be no university, no marriage.' Fred sighed. 'What I'd give to see the world, Princess Caraboo. I would swap my life with yours at the drop of a hat.' He gazed into the fire, which crackled and spat.

She knew he didn't mean that. He had no idea what it was like to live on the road, to sleep hungry, to have nothing.

She swallowed. She must remember who she was at all times. Princess Caraboo, daughter of the South Seas. Regal huntress and ruler-to-be of Javasu. Not Mary Willcox, country maid ruined twice over, beggar.

She offered him the pigeon to set over the fire.

'You are so clever,' he said, taking it, now flattened and pinned ready for cooking and propped it over the embers.

Caraboo inspected her own bird. *Clever*. Nobody had ever called her that.

'Din-ner!' she said.

'Dinner,' Fred repeated. His hand was still bleeding, and he saw her looking at it. 'It's nothing,' he said. 'Honestly.'

'Honestly?' Caraboo said.

'True,' he said, and his lips made a most pleasant shape when he said the word, she thought.

She sat up straight. She was supposed to be beguiling him, she reminded herself.

Caraboo took her pigeon off the fire, cut it in two and gave half to Fred. It tasted delicious.

'The best food and the best company,' he said. 'I salute you, Princess. I should never have doubted you.'

No, you shouldn't.

'There is no side to you, unlike English girls, who preen and play the idiot.' He turned the second pigeon over so that it cooked on the other side. 'I only wish I knew what you were saying to me.' He paused. 'Something tells me you think I am an idiot.'

Caraboo said nothing.

'I think, perhaps, you know a lot more than you say. You know, I used to think Mama a fool for all her interests, her books, her anthropology – rather than sewing or music like most mothers. But you have opened my eyes a little . . .'

He looked at his cut, which was still bleeding. 'I should bind it up, I suppose.'

She took his hand in hers; his skin was softer than her own. All the men she had ever known had working hands, calloused and hard, not smooth as the skin on milk like his. The blood was trickling down towards his palm.

'Really, it's nothing,' he insisted.

But before she knew it, she had taken his hand in her mouth and sucked the wound.

If she had thought about it beforehand, she would never have done it. If she had asked herself what Fred's reaction would be, she would never have believed it.

The second her mouth touched his skin, he pulled

away from her, stammering apologies. Frederick Worrall, ladies' man, seducer, was blushing. Caraboo turned away and took a breath. Was he disgusted by her? What did it mean? For the first time, as Princess Caraboo, she felt nervous. This man, this dandy, hated women and hated her, didn't he? Oh! She had shown herself as nothing but a fool!

She had made Fred Worrall flush; she knew her own heart was pounding triple time. Perhaps she should run away, swim back now—

At that second, the second pigeon caught fire. Fred jumped up and took it off, but it was too late: the little thing was blackened and shrivelled, a burned offering. Caraboo looked at Fred, a mess from head to foot, holding a charred pigeon on a stick . . . She had truly never seen anything so ridiculous. She couldn't help laughing out loud, which was most unprincesslike. In that moment Fred must have realized how he looked, and he laughed too. He took a burned twig, drew some patterns on his face and arms and began to dance, the burned bird held high; finally he sat down, still chuckling.

Now Princess Caraboo got up to dance – not a silly dance like Fred's, and not with her knife, in case she gave him any further cause for alarm. She danced, and after a while she forgot that Frederick Worrall was even there.

'Magnificent,' he said, clapping, and Caraboo turned to glance at him. Did he mean it? She reminded herself that she didn't care, and sat down again. Fred still looked rather ridiculous, with his dirty, smudgy face.

'Ah, you don't approve, Princess?' he said. 'So you won't have me in your tribe after all . . . Look, I'm sorry I jumped away like that before – you know, with the hand,' he said.

Caraboo hoped she showed no emotion.

'I didn't expect it. Cass always said that you didn't like being touched and, well, that you didn't like men. So, I was . . .' He shook his head. 'I wasn't expecting it. Not from you. Not at all.'

Caraboo cocked her head on on side.

'Caraboo, I want to be friends.' Fred's face, under smears of charcoal and blood, was as open and as beautiful as any face she had ever seen.

'Friends?' he said again. And held out his hand for her to shake.

Caraboo nodded. 'Friends, yes . . .'

She hesitated, looking at his hand, his face. His eyes. She remembered how he had reacted when she put his hand to her mouth. Had it been disgust? She thought not. Her heart, she realized, was pounding.

She took his hand, but instead of shaking it, simply clasped it in her own, and before she knew what she was doing she had leaned forward to press her lips to his, charcoal-smeared but soft. She felt him hold his breath, and for a moment she did too, but then he was kissing her back, cautious and careful – not like she had imagined a man like him would be. He smelled of fire and pigeon's blood and warm, clean sweat.

His fingers brushed her shoulder, uncertain, and then they were gone – he was still not sure if he could touch her, she realized. She felt a strange fluttering in her chest, and for a moment she wanted to pull him to her, to show him he could—

Suddenly she drew back. She had forgotten herself.

Fred Worrall was looking at her with wide blue eyes. She could tell that he was not disgusted at all.

What had she done?

She quickly got up and ran to the water's edge so that he wouldn't see her face.

Princess Caraboo never blushed.

She stepped into the water and swam as fast as she could, telling herself that all was as it should be; that this had been how she intended it to go, all along. But she still felt warm in spite of the cold water: she could still feel her lips where Fred's lips had touched them, and she knew, in her heart, that it was not what she had planned at all.

*

Caraboo went back to the house and changed. She thought she would spend some time in the library, even produce the handwriting samples for Mrs Worrall – anything to stop herself thinking about the feel of Fred's mouth and the look in Fred's eyes; about how her plan had somehow been turned topsy turvy.

She did not notice Captain Palmer: he suddenly appeared in the first-floor corridor, out of nowhere, and caught her by the arm so tightly that she could not reach for her knife. He pulled her close, and even at this early hour his breath was thick with rum and tobacco. Caraboo tried to pull away, to summon up the image of the leopard growling beside her, but it eluded her. She was trapped, alone.

'All right, Princess?' The captain spoke low, his manner completely changed. Ice cold, and hard, not the jolly sailor any more. 'Nobody's here,' he whispered, 'so you just keep it quiet as you like.'

Caraboo said nothing. If she had bothered to examine her thoughts, she had been prepared for some kind of conversation like this. But she had pushed the idea away. She did not want to think about what Captain Palmer might want from her.

She drew herself up: she had been a princess long before this wretched excuse for a man had said so aloud.

'You play it like that, lady, but I'm no fool,' he said.

'I know you're hokey. Princess, my salty arse! But if that's what her ladyship here wants, that's what we'll give 'er, see?'

Caraboo cursed silently. She should have known that a man, any man, would want something, would not be content, as she was, just to pretend; just to be someone else.

The captain drew even closer – she could almost taste his stinking breath. 'I don't know who you are, or what your lay is, but if you're royalty, I'm Horatio Nelson.' His eyes glittered, his fingers dug hard into her arm. 'But we can get along, you and me. We can be useful to each other. Are you here on the nab, lady? What are you after?' He gripped her even more tightly and she tried to suppress a gasp. She wanted to shout, to yell, to tell him that Caraboo was no thief, but she couldn't. She had to be brave, to be strong. 'You can tell old Captain Palmer,' he said.

She glared at him. He whispered into her ear: she could feel the flecks of spit on her skin and felt a wave of sickness come over her.

'I think we can make our fortune with this little play,' the captain said. 'Here or on the fairgrounds – you the Princess, me your interpreter. I haven't set my plan in stone, but you'll go along with it, or I'll drop you in it. Head first into the fire, lady.'

Caraboo felt her heart speed up, hammering so loud she thought it would burst.

'So play along, lady, and remember – if you leave before I'm good and ready, I will find you.' He traced a line across her throat and she felt her legs give way. She put one hand out against the wall to steady herself.

'I will find you and I will make you pay.' The captain looked her up and down, and all the bones in her legs turned to jelly. 'In every way possible.' He shook her off.

At that moment Phoebe came bustling past and the captain's manner changed, like the sun coming out from behind a cloud. He laughed, as if Caraboo had just said something amusing.

'Come along, Princess!' he said, exactly like a jolly uncle, or the good-hearted seafaring war hero everyone knew him to be.

But Caraboo stood there, frozen.

7

GONE AWRY

Knole Park House
May 1819

'Miss Cassandra.' He said her name, deep and low,
like a moan. Cassandra kissed him again. She knew
she was desirable – she had seen it reflected in the faces
of quite a few young men in Bath. But she thought
she had never felt it so strongly, never felt so utterly
adored. He wanted her so much it made her dizzy with
the power of it. She looked up into the trees where the
light came through in moving diamonds, and felt
happier than ever. Since she'd begun meeting Will, and
welcomed Caraboo into her life, Knole had become
almost bearable.

She lay back against the soft mossy tree trunk, Will's
jacket folded up beneath her head, his body pressed hard
against hers. She was tingling all over, as if every nerve

ending sparkled with that same electricity Professor Heyford used in his beastly experiments.

Will closed his eyes as if in pain, and rolled away.

'Will? Is everything all right? Will?'

'This is not right. I shouldn't . . . you are too perfect,' he said, looking away. 'You deserve everything . . . everything in the world . . .'

Cassandra picked a handful of grass and threw it at him. 'Will! I have everything I need. I have your complete adoration . . . don't I?'

He turned back. 'You know that.'

She reached out a hand. 'Yes, I do.'

'Miss Cassandra . . .'

'Look at me, Will.' She took his face in her hands, tracing the outline; she felt him shudder when her fingertip touched his lips.

'Oh, I love you, Miss Cassandra,' he sighed. 'So much.'

Cassandra smiled. 'Then everything is exactly as it should be.' She kissed him.

'I promise you, Miss Cassandra, even if it takes me two, three years, I will ask your father. Then, when we are married—'

'Two years!' Cassandra's mouth turned down in a pout. 'Will, I am bound to *die* if I have to wait two *weeks*! I want to be with you *now*!' She held him close and looked across the meadow towards the park, where Knole glittered white like a tiny sugar palace.

'But, Miss Cassandra—'

She put a finger to his lips. 'Cassandra. No "Miss" when we are together.'

'I want to do right by you and your family. I have nothing,' Will said. 'I am an innkeeper's son . . .'

'You could be a chimney sweep for all I care. I am sixteen! We could go abroad. The Alps! Italy! Mary Shelley went to—'

'Mary Shelley?' Will said, making a face.

Cassandra waved a hand. 'She is a lady novelist – she wrote *Frankenstein* when she was just eighteen! . . .'

Will coughed. 'I was thinking, perhaps, of America. There are so many opportunities there, Captain Palmer—'

Cassandra sat up. 'Mama's family is from America. From Philadelphia. She has never wanted to return—'

'But we would be together,' Will said. 'In America no one cares who your father is. We could have a place of our own, an inn that serves travellers and traders . . .'

Cassandra sighed heavily. 'Mama says that America is backward in art and fashion, and not in the least picturesque.'

Will took a deep breath. 'But, Miss Cassandra, you don't know what it's like to be poor. In America I could earn my fortune, then you could follow me. If we both leave now, it'll be hard. You've never had to live without money—'

'I don't care about money, Will!' She didn't want to hear about America. She clung to him, and felt his heart beating, louder than a volley of rifles under his shirt.

'Truly, Cassandra?'

She kissed him again. She had had quite enough of talking.

'Caraboo! Princess Caraboo!' Mrs Worrall stood on the steps that led out of the library and down towards the park. Caraboo could not fail to hear her, but she didn't move. She was in the library, hidden in the window seat, curtain drawn tight so none might see her, one of Mrs Worrall's books lying open upon her lap. She had spent all the previous day avoiding everyone. She had planned to spend the day on the island, but the thought that Captain Palmer might follow her and catch her alone, made her shiver.

She should have realized that she was betraying her secret by letting him interpret Caraboo. She had put herself in his hands and could not see a way out.

She had tried to clear her mind, to think of some plan to get a head start out of Knole, before the captain found out that she was gone. But as yet she had none. She had not been able to concentrate on anything – even the words on the page swam in front of her eyes – and when she shut them, all she could see was Captain Palmer's face, all she could smell was the foul stink of liquor on his breath.

Caraboo would have to be killed off – she would have to become somebody else; someone the captain would never find . . .

Her plans for Fred Worrall seemed childish now. What had happened with him on the island, merely a few days ago, felt like a lifetime away.

She heard the doors open, and froze.

'Ah, Professor Heyford!' Mrs Worrall said, and Caraboo relaxed a little.

'Madam?'

'I wonder if you had seen my latest addition to the library? My *Pantographia*?'

'No, madam, though I admit I should like to.'

'Perhaps Fred or the captain has spirited it away. I do so wish they would leave books on the shelf where they found them!'

'Quite so,' the professor agreed.

Caraboo thought that Mary Willcox would have called Professor Heyford a regular needy mizzler, a right royal suck-up.

'And the captain? Have you seen him? I would so prefer to talk to the both of you at once.'

Caraboo felt sick simply hearing the man mentioned.

'I think the captain is, ah, resting.' Professor Heyford cleared his throat. 'If I may be so bold, Mrs Worrall, I think Captain Palmer is a little too fond of his drink.'

'He is a naval man – it is the way of things in the navy, I think – at least, that is what Mr Worrall tells me. If you had seen half of what he has experienced across the world . . . Has he told you of those spirits, those blood-sucking harpies, the Penanggalan?'

'More than once, actually, Mrs Worrall.'

'Well, there you are! The man is a marvel,' she said. 'I had nightmares for three whole nights after hearing that story. Well, then, if he is not here, I will at least tell you, Professor . . .' She paused and Caraboo listened. Perhaps she might hear something useful.

'See!' Mrs Worrall went on excitedly. 'I have a letter from Mr Gutch at the *Bristol Advertiser*. He has heard of Caraboo and he wants to visit our princess here at Knole! This weekend! Marvellous, isn't it? Caraboo is so exciting, Mr Gutch says he would like to write about her, fancy that! And I have had a wonderful idea! I have already sent out some other invitations, after all. I wonder – are there perhaps any of your fellow academics who would like to meet an authentic Javan princess?'

'Yes, yes.' Professor Heyford sounded enthusiastic. 'I do have an acquantaince in London who is measuring native people's brains—'

'Surely Princess Caraboo's brain is currently in use, sir.'

Professor Heyford laughed. 'Of course, madam, of course, but if – when – she dies, he would be first in line to explore that organ. Did you know, Mrs Worrall, that the English brain is always twice the weight and quality of any native one?'

'Is that so, Professor?'

'Oh yes. It is on account of the amount of roast beef consumed in these islands. And naturally, a male brain is larger and more complex than a woman's . . .'

Mrs Worrall harrumphed at that.

'One cannot argue with fact,' the professor said.

A party. Acadmics and newspapermen gawking and clucking at her. Princess Caraboo felt her heart sink. She was like a butterfly pinned behind glass. This should never have happened. Caraboo was a dream, a marsh light, something that almost existed but not quite. A story, a legend – not a truth to be dissected and picked over.

She opened the window and slipped away into the

park. She looked up at the house, the rows of windows reflecting the afternoon sun. If that man was there in the house, drunk, then he could not come after her. She looked again, hand shading her eyes to see better. Was there some movement behind a window on the second floor? Perhaps he was there, watching her, this very moment. Perhaps his drunkenness was just assumed.

Caraboo was relieved to find Cassandra down by the lake, looking at the sparkling light on the water. She was uncharacteristically quiet, even thoughtful.

Caraboo sat down beside her; she felt safer in company.

'Caraboo?' Cassandra plucked a long blade of grass and twisted it in her fingers. 'I know you must have been through some scrapes. I cannot imagine pirates!' She paused. 'I was wondering . . . do you know what it is like to be poor?'

The Princess looked perplexed. Even if she could understand every word – and of course Caraboo's English was supposed to be getting better – how would a princess understand poverty? True, when she had been on the road she'd had nothing. But that was different – until that moment when she had fallen down in a faint on the road outside Almondsbury, she had been somebody else entirely.

'I do not think I would mind so very much,'

Cassandra said. 'Being poor, I mean. Especially if one is discovering new landscapes and so on.'

Caraboo babbled back in Javasu, saying that she did not think that one could eat or wear new landscapes. She warned Cassandra that new landscapes might contain most unpleasant people.

'I so wish I could understand you, Princess,' Cassandra sighed. 'He loves me, I know it, and sometimes I am sure that I love him . . .'

Caraboo set her face in what she hoped was an expression of mild concern. This was one of the things she enjoyed most about being Caraboo: listening. Perhaps Cassandra's worries could help her forget her own, for the time being.

'He talks only of America.' Cassandra paused, frowning. 'Darling Will, he wants to go alone all the way across the world to make his fortune, and come back for me when it is done. But I will not sit alone in Knole Park for years until he returns. I wanted to go with him, but not there. Why can't he make his fortune in Italy or Greece? Somewhere beautiful, classical. I used to think we were so alike, so perfectly matched. Oh, I know he works hard, but I do too, in my own way – at my needlework, for one thing.'

Caraboo kept quiet. She had never seen Cassandra work at anything except her own delight.

'And I know what love is – I have read so many novels. Those feelings that sweep you off your feet . . . The electricity – I feel it with him . . .'

At the word 'electricity' Caraboo began an angry babble.

Cassandra smiled. 'No, not like that, Princess!' She paused, threw a stalk of grass out into the water and watched it float away. 'But if I loved him, wouldn't I want everything he wants? Wouldn't I want to be in America with him, an innkeeper's wife?'

Caraboo looked away. This place was almost perfect, she thought, yet both Cassandra and Fred longed for somewhere else, to live like some*one* else.

'When he is here with me' – Cassandra took Caraboo's hands in hers – 'I believe it, I truly do. I think – and I read this in a novel once – he touches my soul!' Her eyes were round with wonder. 'But when he is gone and I think of us together, in Boston, or New York, or any of those dreary, fountainless American cities, I only imagine the smell that was in the Golden Bowl; if I breathe in deeply when my arms are around his neck I can smell it: old beer and tobacco and slops.'

Her shoulders drooped and she shook her head. 'I do not want that, Princess. I know that I do not . . . even' – she lowered her voice – 'even with Will.' She sighed again. 'Love shouldn't be a bore, should it?'

Caraboo said nothing. Poor Will; Cassandra would break his heart without art or guile, only by believing – sometimes – that she did love him. Perhaps she herself should be taking lessons from Cassandra.

She looked across the fields towards the village and felt guilty. Why had she encouraged their affair? Will was a good man . . . well, what she knew of him was good, but hadn't Captain Palmer proved there was no trusting anybody?

Cassandra had got up, brushing the grass off her dress. Caraboo wondered whether she had brushed away Will Jenkins almost as quickly.

Oh, Caraboo knew that Will would get over Cassandra. It might take him longer than it had taken Cassandra, but he was good looking enough. And he was an innkeeper's son – he had more backing than a Cambridge fortune . . . which was, after all, the only fortune Caraboo had. And that, as anyone fluent in London cant knew, was no fortune at all.

The Princess watched Cassandra walk ahead of her with that carefree step that only money could buy. If she had money, she could be away from Knole in the blink of an eye. She could be in America, a land so big no one was certain where the end of it lay. Captain Palmer would not follow, surely, if she was on a ship a thousand miles from here. Perhaps that was the answer for her.

Get herself to Bristol and . . . and what? Caraboo cursed under her breath: to raise the passage to America would take much more than anything she could trade . . .

Cassandra turned round. 'Princess, I fear I have infected you with my low spirits! Forgive my mood. I should count my blessings, and be light-hearted, and not mope over Will Jenkins, who has, sadly, no idea of novels at all. He may kiss me like a gentleman, but I cannot wait in hope while he gets himself to and from America, can I?'

Caraboo merely smiled. What else could she do?

Cassandra gasped as she recollected something. 'I almost forgot to pass on the good news! Mama has agreed to a party! Well, she doesn't call it a party herself but that is what it amounts to! We shall all be excused any boredom for at least one night! A party!' She danced around in a circle to illustrate the word, then pulled Caraboo after her. 'There will be music and dancing – I told her you can't simply have a deal of dry old lectures without the sweetener that is music. And what's more, she has promised to invite Diana – I have told you all about her – and the Greshams will be coming too. You will have a chance to meet Edmund, who is very, very handsome. You know, if I call up Edmund's face, I cannot say which is the fairer, him or Will . . . If Edmund looks too long at you, I know I shall be jealous!' Cassandra looked away. 'Dear, dear Princess Caraboo! What must you think of me?!' She frowned. 'I do care for Will, you know. He has made my life more bearable in so many ways.' She turned and began to run back up the slope to the house. 'And we will make you a special outfit for the party – Mama has promised. It will be such fun!'

Caraboo followed Cassandra slowly towards the house. She thought of staying out, but the sun was low and she didn't want to be outside on her own. Her leopard seemed to have left her side for good. The world was conspiring against the Princess, boxing her into a corner like a sheep in a pen ready for the shearer. As she neared the terrace in front of the house she spotted Captain Palmer, Professor Heyford and Frederick Worrall. Were they waiting for her? The captain would not try anything with witnesses around, would he? She straightened up. She would do her best not to let any of them see how scared she was.

'Mama, I've looked everywhere – the Princess must be out.' Fred came into the library. He hadn't seen Caraboo since the day before and was rather worried. Was she avoiding him?

'Fred – look, there she is, with Cassandra.' Mrs Worrall opened the doors that led out onto the terrace. Fred saw the girls coming towards the house, Cassandra in front, skipping along, Caraboo walking behind her, slow and stately, as if she owned every inch of the earth under her feet. He could see now that perhaps part of her stangeness, her otherness, was to do with nobility. He closed his eyes for a moment and remembered her doubled up with laughter . . . her warm kiss. Was that the same girl?

'All is ready, Professor, is it not?' Mrs Worrall bustled over to the writing desk set up by the window.

Fred watched the girls. They were such a pair of opposites, Cass so English and fair, Caraboo browner than a hazelnut, walking barefoot across the stone flags.

'Mrs Worrall thought it a grand idea to send a sample of the Princess's handwriting off to Oxford,' Professor Heyford said. He didn't sound happy about it.

'Yes, there is a specialist there, in linguistics,' Mrs Worrall told him.

Fred thought he could almost hear Professor Heyford grinding his teeth.

'I don't know if she'll take to it, madam – you can never be sure with these island people . . .'

Captain Palmer was sitting in a leather chair in the corner. A full decanter of what Fred guessed was rum rested on a side table at his elbow. He poured himself a glass.

'Cassandra! Princess!' Mrs Worrall saluted Caraboo, hand to forehead, and she saluted back, then turned to the professor and, finally, Fred. He looked her in the eye; she didn't look away, and Fred wondered if she was angry. Why couldn't he read her face? He knew what Cassandra was thinking before she opened her mouth, and any other girl – well, Letty! He turned away. He didn't want to think about her now.

'Princess! My dear Caraboo.' Mrs Worrall steered her over to the writing desk.

'Oh, the handwriting!' Cassandra said. She turned to Caraboo too, and made writing shapes in the air.

Fred watched and wondered how Caraboo did not laugh – a room full of nominally sane adults describing circles in the air. He himself could not help but smile at the picture. How odd, he thought, to be the Princess, so cut off from everything. To float above a situation, to be the centre of attention yet, at one and the same moment, completely separate.

Caraboo looked at him for a second and – had he imagined it? – he swore he saw a sadness in her eyes.

'I will demonstrate, my dear.' Mrs Worrall picked up the pen, dipped it carefully in the inkwell, and then wrote, in curling copperplate letters, *Princess Caraboo*. 'There,' she said, pointing to the words, and then to Caraboo. 'Prin-cess Cara-boo.' Then she wrote the letters of the alphabet down the side of the page, making the sound as she went.

'Mrs Worrall, madam' – the captain drained his glass – 'I don't think our princess will take to this at all.'

'We can but try,' Mrs Worrall replied.

The captain spoke to Caraboo, and Fred saw the Princess lower her eyes. Was he telling her off? He strained to listen for the slightest inflection, the variation of tone that might tell him something of what was being said. He cursed his lack of interest in Greek or Latin.

'Here, Princess.' Mrs Worrall pressed the pen into Caraboo's hand and motioned for her to sit.

She dipped the pen in the ink, looking not to the captain but to Mrs Worrall for guidance.

'That's it, dear!'

Caraboo put pen to paper. The nib split and the ink came out in a blob.

'You see, madam, in the East they write with brushes.'

'You would prefer a brush, Princess?' Mrs Worrall said slowly.

Caraboo ignored everyone. Fred watched as she tried again, scratching the paper roughly at first, trying to copy Mrs Worrall's writing. The concentration made her forehead gather into furrows. She tried her own name first.

'There, that's as good as you'll get, no doubt.'

Why, wondered Fred, was the captain so against this exercise?

'But, Captain, I think our princess shows some aptitude.' Professor Heyford grinned, happy to be bettering his rival for once. 'Why don't you ask the Princess to write something in her own tongue for us?'

'Yes, yes!' Mrs Worrall clapped her hands.

'Madam—' the captain began.

'Look, Mama, I think she is!' Cassandra said. Caraboo was drawing a series of strange and beautiful curlicues.

'I say.' Professor Heyford took off his glasses and cleaned them, to get a better look. 'Astounding! It's almost . . .'

'Almost what, Professor?' Fred could see that his mother was thrilled.

'Somewhere between Arabic and Chinese,' the professor said.

The captain got up, and suddenly the Princess stopped writing. Palmer walked over to the writing desk and Fred swore he saw Caraboo tense, just a little. For a second he thought the captain might even spill his drink over the writing as he looked at it.

'Ah well, the Arab traders, they came through the South Seas, you know, Ibn Battuta . . .'

'Pardon?' Mrs Worrall said.

The captain returned to his high-backed leather chair, drained his second glass of rum and began a tale of some Arabian explorer.

The Princess got up to leave. Fred wanted to follow her, but she caught his eye and shook her head. He had definitely done something to offend her. The kiss . . . But *she* had started it, not him.

'Princess flown the coop?' The captain pushed himself up off the chair and went out too.

Mama, Cass and Professor Heyford were all marvelling over the Princess's handwriting, with the professor nodding and smiling. 'Most definitely the Javasu dialect.'

Fred left the room, taking his glass onto the terrace as the sun dipped golden over the lake. There was the island, just as it had been yesterday. Knole too was exactly the same.

Fred felt the rum burn the back of his throat. It was him that was different. The boy he'd been when he left London seemed like someone else now . . . He shook his head. Edmund would have laughed at him.

He turned and looked up at the great house. He could stay here his whole life if he wished – go up to university for a couple of years, follow Father into the bank. He sighed. He knew there was so much more to life than this. He walked round to the front door, his feet crunching on the gravel, and it was then that he saw something, up on the first floor. In Caraboo's room, the one next to his sister's, Captain Palmer was shutting the curtain, the look on his face thunderous. Fred ducked behind the beech tree so he wouldn't be seen. He ran into the house and up the stairs, but by the time he reached the first floor he saw the captain coming back along the corridor, nodding to him as if everything were normal. Fred felt the relief wash over him. What had he been thinking? How stupid.

He went up to the Princess's door and raised his hand as if to knock. But then he thought he heard something . . . He pressed his ear against the panel, strained to listen. There. He could hear something, he was sure.

Tiny muffled sobs.

8

CAPTURED IN OILS

Knole Park House
May 1819

Fred did not go down for breakfast the next morning.
For the very first time in his eighteen years he was at a
loss as to what to do next. Edmund, if he knew – and
Fred thanked the Lord he did not – would laugh enough
to shake his bones. Fred leaned over the banister at
the top of the stairs and saw Finiefs let in Mr Barker,
the artist,. He could not bear to go down and join his
Mother in glad-handing and smiling.

He sighed. He knew Ed would suggest having it
out with the fellow, fists up in the corridor. Or even
better, let Finiefs deal with him and throw him out.
And that had been his instinct, after hearing Caraboo
sobbing like that, so quietly, so sadly. The thought of
what he had done afterwards made him flush, and

he turned away, trying to block it out . . .

Fred had hared after the captain, who, after a shaky few days, now moved as nimbly on land as anyone half his age, and found him at last, relaxed as you like, finishing off another decanter of Father's rum and about to tell another tale of the South Seas to Mama.

'The Penanggalan,' the captain said as he refilled his glass, 'is a most terrible thing, madam.'

Mrs Worrall frowned. 'Surely, Captain,' she said, 'such fancies are but native superstitions and folk tales, like our ogres or the Black Dog of legend.'

'Ah, but don't some folk swear blind they've seen them? Didn't I hear of an old man, when I was a boy down in Rye on the coast, whose heart stopped dead after he'd seen that dog? Chased him to his grave, they say . . .'

'Captain Palmer?' Fred said coolly.

The captain drained his glass.

'I wonder if I could speak to you?' Fred paused. 'In private.'

'Fred, darling, the captain was about to begin a tale.'

'I assure you, Mama' – Fred's voice was tight – 'this won't take long.'

Captain Palmer nodded, and Fred waited while he rose unsteadily and made his way over to the door.

If Mama had not been sitting there, Fred thought,

he would have knocked him down there and then.

Once he was in the hall, Fred took the captain's arm and led him out onto the dark terrace.

'You can let go of my arm, young man,' the captain said, trying to pull away.

'Just what are you up to?' Fred slammed him up against the wall. 'I saw you! Outside her room. Are you interfering with her – with the Princess? I ought to have you thrown out this instant!'

The captain said nothing for a moment; then, 'I see.'

'You see what? You see *what* exactly?'

'Keep your powder dry, young man,' he said softly. 'The Princess was merely missing her home island. The sun, the warmth' – he paused – 'her family.'

'It was more than that.' Fred couldn't see Caraboo going to the captain for comfort. Of any kind.

'Oh,' the captain said, looking Fred straight in the eye, 'I think I see where your thoughts are taking you, a fine-looking buck like yourself.'

'Do not refer to me as a buck.'

'Apologies.' The captain backed away.

'What about the Princess?! What is your game, sir?'

'Game?' The captain raised his eyebrows. 'You think *I* play a game, young sir?' He almost smiled. 'And I would wager you'd play your own game too, is that it?'

Fred bridled. 'What do you mean? I am not a ruffian

who makes young women cry, sir—' He checked himself, thinking of Letty and Essie and the others, and looked away.

The captain smiled. 'I am a man of the world; I know a young man's thoughts and how they tack and change. If you would like to see your way to finding me a good silver crown, I'd be more than happy to parley with the Princess on your behalf.' He leaned closer. 'She does not take kindly to being forced into anything, if you get my drift,' he said with a wink.

'Is that what you think?!' Fred was incandescent – but he was also frozen. How did this salt scum know so much about his thoughts?

'She is a looker.'

'She is not like that!'

'How can you know what she is like? Do you speak Javasu, sir? I think not.' The captain shrugged. 'The Princess is just a girl – and, you, if I am not mistaken, like a game girl.'

Fred tried to punch the man, but his fist only connected with the wall behind his head. The pain shot up his arm.

'I am not a fool, so don't play the parson with me, lad, or talk of honour or other foolish niceties.' He lowered his voice and growled, 'I have seen your sort before: second sons – or eldest ones, for that matter – with too much time, money, and a father who is too busy to notice what is under his nose. Now, one silver crown . . . If you wish to spend the night with her, I could fix it for you, but that would be twice the tariff. Now, either pay up or shut up and let's hear no more about it.' The captain started to walk away.

Fred was left standing alone on the terrace, knuckles grazed, mind racing. Could the Princess be bought so easily? Did she know that this was what the captain was up to? Did she condone it? And why did he care so much?

All he could do was shout after the captain, like an idiot, 'I am not a second son!'

Remembering all this made Fred flush with shame. Why had he not thought of something cutting to say? Why had the Princess not been up on the roof this morning? He had spent the hour before and after the sun had risen waiting for her – in vain. Was there something going on between her and the captain after all? Some plot, some scheme?

Then Caraboo, Cassandra and the captain were there, just below him in the hall, curtseying and bowing as Mother introduced them to the artist.

Fred studied the Princess closely: was she not quieter than yesterday? Was there something about the slope of her shoulder that suggested sadness? He noticed that she did not meet the captain's eye once. She did not care for the man at all, he was sure of it. He must have some knowledge, some secret of hers he was using against her. And her dress – it was short, her shoulders plainly visible. Was she not simply a girl of Letty's sort, dressed up and playing some kind of long game? Bamboozled by that soak of a captain?

She was not like that! He would swear it. She was different. He thought of that moment on the island and closed his eyes. When he opened them again, she was staring straight at him. He wanted to tell her that he could help, he was on her side. But she had already turned away, and Mama was laughing at something the artist had said, and the party moved away into the Chinese drawing room, out of sight.

Cassandra put on her second-favourite gown. Phoebe pulled the hem straight as Cassandra admired herself in the mirror.

'You are a picture, Miss Cassandra.'

'Maybe I can persuade Mr Barker to paint me too . . .'

Phoebe smiled. 'The artist? He would be a fool not to, any man would look twice at you, Miss Cassandra. Any man.'

Cassandra did not notice Phoebe's long sigh, and

hurried away downstairs. It was her hope that the artist, Mr Barker, whose reputation in the West Country, she knew, was second to none, would set eyes on her and immediately wish to paint her. But Mr. Barker did not even look up to acknowledge her entrance.

As the morning progressed Cassandra was thoroughly ignored. Caraboo had been posed and posed again. The artist had bought a selection of turbans – golden things adorned with peacock feathers that stood a clear foot above her head.

Eventually he had settled on no turban at all, which Cassandra thought odd.

'The Princess always wears a turban, sir,' she said.

'Hmm, well, her own is made of such dull stuff, it merely sucks in all the light. Bring me a better cloth and she may wear that.' Cassandra frowned, but she sent Phoebe to find something else while Mr Barker stood back, considering her head and shoulders through a frame made from holding his hands in a kind of rectangle shape.

Cassandra could see that Caraboo was not happy; she was nervous, and Cassandra thought it might be because the room was full of people. Mr Barker was more famous than Mr Bird of Bristol, who had painted Diana's family last year. According to Mama, as soon as the word had spread to Bath that a real and genuine Javanese princess was staying with the Worralls at Knole, he had been intrigued by Caraboo's story and wanted to see her.

Mr Barker arranged a piece of cloth about Caraboo's shoulders. Cassandra could see her flinching as he came close. 'Perhaps, sir, you could instruct me as to your wishes? She is nervous of new people.'

'That will not be necessary, miss.' He stood back and addressed Mrs Worrall and the captain. 'I would prefer to work alone. I do not find an audience conducive to any kind of creativity.'

Mrs Worrall looked mildly crushed. 'We shall be quiet, sir,' she said, but he waved her and her daughter away.

Cassandra stalked across the terrace. 'Fred! You are lurking about so, and sulking, I do believe. Are you yet another infected by low spirits this morning?'

'How so?' Fred looked up.

Cassandra leaned close. 'The Princess is not herself, I believe.'

'You think?'

She nodded. 'I had to wake her this morning. It was the first time!' She looked at Fred. 'And what is wrong with you? Have you not received a letter from your love?'

'I do not have a love,' he said, and changed the subject

a little too smartly, Cassandra thought. 'Did the artist send you out?'

Cassandra sighed. 'He did. I was hoping to be included in the portrait, *The Princess Caraboo and Miss Cassandra Worrall of Knole Park* . . .'

She expected her brother to laugh at her, but when she turned, she saw that he had already gone back into the house.

Cassandra walked round to the stables, lifting her skirts well clear of any dirt, and made a fuss of Zephyr.

'Why didn't he paint me, Zeph?' she asked. 'You are the only living creature that understands me.' She rested her head against his neck.

'I thought I did too . . .' The whisper was such a shock that Cassandra nearly pitched over into the horse's bedding.

'Will Jenkins!' she whispered back. 'What in heaven's name brings you here?!'

'I was sent on an errand to the city this morning and thought I would look in on the most beautiful girl in the whole world on the way, and steal a kiss. Or two.'

'We must be careful!' she said. 'Vaughan is near! Anyone might see you!'

'It is worth it . . .' He moved closer.

'Not now!' Cassandra shrank back. 'Please, Will! If we are discovered . . .'

'I am leaving, then,' Will said, stepping away.

She had upset him, she could read it in his face.

'Will, you know I do not enjoy surprises. Please remember that.'

'But America . . . we have plans to make.' He moved closer again. 'I was hoping to depart before the weather turns in the autumn.'

'Will, you must keep your voice low,' she whispered.

'Yes, of course,' he sighed. 'I do love you, Miss Cassandra.' He was looking at her with so much longing it hurt to look back.

'I know you do, Will,' she said.

'Can you keep still please, miss – um, your highness!'

Princess Caraboo could hear the exasperation in the artist's voice. She was doing her best. But her whole body ached from being still these last hours. She thought her short hair must look exceedingly untidy. She was grateful he had not made her wear any of the costumes he had brought with him, but staying still, especially with a piece of fabric draped over her usual hunting dress, was, she thought, close to torture.

The worst of it was that she had nothing to do but think. And all she could think about was Captain Palmer. Why had she allowed that man to shape her story, to speak her language – to gain any hold over her at all? She sighed and the artist swore.

She had never meant any harm to Mrs Worrall or the family – Fred excluded. And even he could not be blamed for being a product of his class, a person who thought the world existed merely to fulfil his every need. And perhaps he was not like that after all . . .

But Captain Palmer . . . He would keep her as a man keeps a dog, to bark and walk and show its paces, or be beaten by a strap. When the handwriting was returned, she was bound to be found out, and then that would be an end to it – but perhaps that end might mean prison! Her heart raced. She had no choice but to run while she had a scrap of freedom left. If she could only get as far as Bristol . . . She shivered.

The artist threw down his brushes. 'That's it! I do believe there is some devil in you that makes you wriggle so!' His tone was unkind, and Caraboo allowed herself to look upset. Then she remembered that she was royalty and drew herself up, throwing the fabric to the floor, snatching up her black turban and mumbling Javasu curses at him as she left.

Caraboo soon regretted this last action, as she was fairly dying to see how the portrait looked. It was a vanity, but she could not imagine any living soul, now or in the future, wanting to paint Mary Willcox of Witheridge, Devon.

And in any case she longed to stretch her legs and get out of the house, even if only for a moment. So she ran across the lawn and down to the lake. She turned for a moment to glance back at the house: Captain Palmer was looking out of the window, plain as day, a ship's glass trained upon her and following her each and every step.

At least if he was in the house he could not be on the island. She made her way to the lakeside and pushed the rowing boat away from the shore. He could not follow her now. She reminded herself that Caraboo was still a princess – she had known it all along, well before he came along with his overblown story of kidnap and pirates. He might have her cornered, but she had to maintain her dignity. At least Captain Palmer didn't know about Mary Willcox, had never so much as heard of her. She held that truth close as she struck out through the water.

But when she stepped onto the island, she knew she was not alone. The path through to her fireplace and altar had been trodden down. Cassandra? No, Caraboo didn't think she could swim. Fred, then? Of course.

She wished she had the kriss on her, but settled for a sharp stick, then made her way as stealthily as she could towards the clearing. Caraboo had wanted to be alone – this was her island, her place . . . except that of course it wasn't. She calmed down. Nothing real belonged to Princess Caraboo.

She shinned up a tree and watched him for a while: he was only half dressed, his wet shirt hanging over a branch as he desperately tried to light a fire. How did the ruling class get to rule when they were all, to a man and woman, so inept?

He cursed, and she had to stifle a laugh. Then he got up and threw his tinderbox on the ground with enough curses to turn the air blue.

Caraboo jumped down, stick raised like a spear, yelling all kinds of Javasu oaths, and Fred Worrall, shocked and stunned, stumbled back into the ashes of the fire, and fell on his backside.

Good, she thought, and stood over him with her spear. He shouldn't be here.

He shuffled backwards. 'Princess! Caraboo, listen! I'm not here to intimidate you.'

Caraboo did not understand 'intimidate'.

'I know about the captain – I know he's put you up to something and I just don't know what it is. Believe me, I want to help.'

Caraboo was wrong-footed. Her heart thumped. What did he know? What had the captain said? She turned away, put down her stick and lit the fire in moments. She sat in front of it, trying to think.

'I heard you last night, crying,' Fred told her.

She ignored him.

'Then I saw you again this morning, and you avoided his eyes. Something happened.'

Caraboo blew at the embers, and the flames burned brighter. She looked at Fred, sitting across from her. He wanted to help. And didn't Caraboo need all the help she could get?

'Captain no good,' she said.

'Exactly!' Fred said. 'That's it exactly, Caraboo. I believe you – I know he's crooked.'

'Caraboo no crooked,' she said firmly.

'No, I don't believe you are.'

She felt a wave of relief wash over her, and smiled at him. There was a twinge, a pang of something else – guilt, perhaps – but she was doing everyone a favour by leaving. And wouldn't she have left days ago now, if she'd had her way?

Fred had brought two fish wrapped in cloth, and she took them and cooked them in the ashes – enveloped in leaves, the way Mary Willcox had seen her father do one summer a long time ago in Devon.

'Caraboo go,' she said as she turned them over. 'Caraboo need go.'

Fred looked at her. 'Perhaps. But wouldn't it be better if the captain went?'

Caraboo looked blank.

'Captain go,' Fred said.

Caraboo looked scared. She stood up and backed away from the fire.

'No, Princess, not with you!' Fred shook his head. 'What I mean is, Caraboo stay, Captain go!'

'Captain stay, Caraboo go,' she said.

'Perhaps I can get the captain so completely drunk . . .' He mimed drinking and then falling over.

Caraboo shook her head. Rum was water to the captain. She made her fingers into a little person, called it Caraboo and made the finger-person climb onto a horse and gallop away. 'Caraboo go – far.'

'I wish you could talk to me, Caraboo,' Fred said. 'I wish you wanted to stay.'

She turned away. Fred sighed. She didn't understand at all, he thought.

'Fred help,' he said at last, leaning so close that she could feel his breath on her cheek. She looked at him, then bent down until her lips brushed his. The Princess felt herself melt into him. Thought of nothing but his touch, his fingertips tracing circles on her neck, his mouth on hers—

Up in the trees a magpie rasped out a call and the Princess Caraboo remembered who she was and leaped away.

She studied Fred: he was completely and utterly lost. She had done it! Her heart was galloping against her ribs – the Princess told herself that it meant nothing. No doubt Fred's beat all the faster.

She smiled.

When Caraboo returned to the house, Mr Barker, the artist, had gone. In the library, Mrs Worrall was reading, while Cassandra sewed and Captain Palmer nursed a glass of rum and looked daggers at her.

'Oh, Princess, if you had seen your portrait!' Mrs Worrall beamed. 'Mr Barker says he will work on it and you are to visit his studio in Bristol on Friday. Fancy that – a real artist's studio!'

Caraboo knew she was dripping on the marble floor, but this was almost too good to be true. *Bristol*, she thought. The city – this was her chance, served up to her on a plate. However, she kept her face blank. Mrs Worrall mimed an artist, and she smiled.

'Yes, and we shall make a day of it,' Cassandra said. 'Mama and I will visit the milliner's, and Captain Palmer says he will come along and translate!'

Mrs Worrall took Caraboo's hand. 'Oh, you are so cold and wet, Princess; do warm yourself or you'll catch a chill.'

'Oh yes, Mama, poor Caraboo – but we shall have

such fun in the city! Perhaps Fred could come with us and we might show Caraboo some of the sights after Mr Barker has finished his work?'

'A wonderful idea!'

Caraboo saluted and went upstairs to change. So the captain would be coming too. No matter. She could lose him in the city a thousand times over. She would only need a change of clothes, ordinary clothes, and she could vanish into the stew in a flash. And if any kind of diversion was needed, Fred would help. Hadn't he said so?

She lay back on her bed and took a deep breath. It would be all right after all.

9

THE LIBERTY OF THE CITY

Mr Barker's Studio
Bristol
May 1819

On the morning of the trip to Bristol, Fred had still not found a moment to talk to Caraboo. The whole household was up early. Mrs Worrall was in a flap about the lectures and dinner party this coming weekend, to which it seemed she had invited half the county. Lady Gresham and Edmund would be arriving for supper this evening, so they had to be back at Knole for six.

Mrs Worrall had arranged to borrow the Edgecombes' cook, who was expected to prepare the mountain of fancies necessary for such an enterprise. Mrs Bridgenorth was in a huff on account of it, and consequently the breakfast eggs were cold.

'Bridgenorth!' Mrs Worrall complained. 'Bring up some of the fruit preserves. I simply cannot abide cold boiled eggs!'

Fred smiled. 'I'll have yours, Mama.'

'And, Fred, you will be sure to meet us at lunch time, at your father's office?'

'Of course, Mama.' He did not tell her that he planned to spend the morning in the Admiralty office or round the docks, hoping to dish up some dirt on Captain Palmer.

'And if you are there before your sister and me, be polite – remember he only thinks of your future.'

'Of course, Mama ... but you know, I was thinking ... I might do as Edmund plans, and take time for a tour. I am not sure about university.'

'For Heaven's sake, Fred, do not mention such foolishness to Mr Worrall! A tour is out of the question! You have a place at Oxford waiting for you in the autumn. I will hear no more about it.'

Cassandra made a face at him across the table.

'And, Cassandra, remember Edmund Gresham will be here tonight. I expect you to behave like a lady, not a street urchin.'

Captain Palmer stirred close to a dozen spoonfuls of sugar into his coffee. 'Ah, now, Mrs Worrall,' he said, leaning back in his chair. 'Lads Mr Fred's age – they have a natural sort of hankering after the world. I have seen it before, many times.'

'Not in this family, Captain Palmer.' She smiled a tight smile and sipped her tea. 'Fred is off to Oxford and that is that.'

Fred couldn't bear to look at Captain Palmer's smug face any longer and went up to his room to dress. It would always be the same. His life had been mapped out: school, university, the bank. He looked out of the window and saw that Vaughan was readying the coach in the stable yard. He felt trapped.

Cassandra kept Vaughan waiting while she changed her tippet twice. Caraboo, Fred noticed, was very quiet; she was dressed in her hunting outfit and turban and was still barefoot, even though Mrs Worrall had suggested sandals might be advisable for the city. She refused to take the kriss, but carried one of the kitchen knives tucked into her belt. Only Captain Palmer, who filled a hipflask full of rum in lieu of any food, seemed calm, Fred thought.

He waited until the coach had left the drive before he got the stable boy to saddle his bay mare. He could reach Bristol with hours to spare before lunch and he didn't have to rely on the road, rutted and hard as it was bound to be. He was bound to find something or other on Captain Palmer, and if he could get shot of the man, Fred thought, kicking the mare into a brisk trot, then Caraboo would see that he meant well. Since he couldn't talk to her, his actions would have to speak for themselves.

Princess Caraboo was grateful for the fact that the captain had no option but to sit outside with the driver. The thought of spending an hour pressed close to the man, as the carriage rocked and jolted into town, had kept her awake all night.

No, she told herself, it was not simply that. She had been planning how to take her leave – thinking of a million and one ways in which she might escape from under the captain's nose and lose herself in the city. She had no change of dress or shoes, her reasoning being that the captain might be less on his guard if she seemed entirely artless.

As they approached Bristol, Caraboo found her spirits lifting. She had been at Knole Park for two months and had quite forgotten about the world outside. They passed people on the road – pedlars, knife-sharpeners, fruit-sellers, then shops and workshops, wheelwrights and smiths, the smells of smoke and work and real life.

Mrs Worrall and Cassandra got out first: Mrs Worrall had a list as long as her arm of things she needed to buy for the party before she visited the milliner's. Caraboo sat up straight as Captain Palmer tipped his hat to the ladies and slid into the seat next to her. He leaned close – Caraboo reckoned if she'd had a light she could have ignited his breath, it was so completely and utterly malodorous.

'We must make plans,' the captain said evenly. Caraboo said nothing; she tried to move away but he sat so close that she was pressed against the side of the carriage.

'I know you understand me, Miss whoever you are – I tried my damnedest to warn you off that writing lark. Even all those professors old Ma Worrall writes to can't be as cotton-headed as Heyford. Our goose is cooked. Our clock is running down, do you see? I'd give it five days – thank the Lord for the party, then there'll be enough of those county nobs that one or two choice items going missing won't matter here or there.'

'Caraboo no steal!' The Princess had never intended to take anything from the Worralls. She had only wanted a place to stay.

'Too late, girlie,' the captain said. 'My time is money. Then we can hightail it north and make ourselves a penny or two on the fairgrounds over the summer; they won't have heard of you up there.'

Caraboo looked daggers. 'No,' she said. 'No fairs! No stealing!'

'Well, that's where we part company, lady. And that's where you're wrong.' He looked at her, grinning. 'See, if you don't, I'll pin the thievery on you, and instead of a few months round the fairs you'll be spending your time locked up in the dark.'

Caraboo shut her eyes. *Worse and worse*, she thought.

'Oh, I don't know why you're sulking, lady,' the captain went on. 'I don't doubt that being Princess Caraboo is a lot easier than being whoever you really are, having that young gentleman follow you around, gawping at you like some lovesick dog.'

She hid her shock. Was it that obvious? What if someone else at Knole had noticed? Caraboo looked away, humming softly to herself. She didn't want to listen to Captain Palmer any more, especially when she knew that what he said was true.

'I know you heard me, so there it is: keep your mouth shut and prattle all that trash for three more days till Mrs Worrall's guests go, then so will we.' The captain smiled, showing teeth that were deep brown, like rum; then put his hand upon her thigh.

She slapped it away immediately. He made her feel sick, but she had to keep her wits sharp today. She was trying to keep a map in her mind and work out the lay of the city, but she did not want Palmer to divine from her face that today was the last day on earth for the

Princess Caraboo. After today, she prayed, she would never have to see Captain Palmer ever again.

The artist's studio was in a building adjoining his house, on the west, and more fashionable, side of town. The light coming in from the north-facing skylights was very bright, and the room smelled strongly of linseed oil and turpentine. There were unfinished canvasses propped up against the wall, mostly portraits – men and women in fine clothes, smiling with their mouths shut.

Mr Barker steered Caraboo towards a chair in the centre of the room. 'And, Captain Palmer,' he said, 'can you please direct the Princess to be still today!'

The captain saluted and burbled in Javasu to Caraboo.

She took off her turban while Captain Palmer looked at the painting, and then sat in a corner and opened his flask – not a very responsible chaperone, Caraboo thought. He began telling Mr Barker how much he would love the South Seas; the ruined temples, the captain promised, were most picturesque.

Princess Caraboo took no notice and concentrated on sitting as still as possible. Back home, many homes ago now, in the life before the South Seas, she had seen portraits in the fine houses in Exeter. And then, in London, even richer people, dressed in all their finery, their hair perfect, their faces free of pockmarks or blemishes that troubled them in life. She couldn't imagine seeing herself like that.

Captain Palmer was still talking. He had been around the world in both directions more than once, he said. Mr Barker said nothing and continued working, only sighing every so often and staring so hard at Caraboo that it was as if he was looking right through her. But after a while, when the captain got on to his tales of disembodied spirits, the artist exploded, throwing his palette to the floor and swearing with old-fashioned West Country obscenities that Caraboo remembered from long ago, when her father, the village cobbler, had injured himself with a hammer.

'Captain Palmer!' Mr Barker said. 'Can you not keep your own counsel? I am trying to work! Go! Now! Take a turn about the garden, walk out to the river, anything! I cannot abide your prattle one moment more!'

Captain Palmer told him that he was required to stay with the girl; that she was a wild one and could not understand English; that he was honour-bound to watch her. But the artist insisted, and had his valet escort the captain out of the house, telling him not to come back until five.

Caraboo tried to keep a straight face. This was even better than she could have hoped. Mr Barker called for a drink of water and told Caraboo she could rest for a moment. She stood up and stretched, arching her back like a cat.

'Come along,' he said. 'Have a look.'

Caraboo went round to the other side of the canvas and could not help gasping.

The portrait was beautiful, in a way she had never thought possible for Mary Willcox, but had always imagined for Caraboo. The girl in the picture, regal in her turban, looked as if she had been painted on the distant shore of some kingdom she ruled, only now brought back to England – so far removed from the girl she had once been, the other girl; the one who had lost a baby, and— No, she would not think of it.

Caraboo smiled. She could walk away from Knole Park and the Worralls now; she could do so knowing that she had not lied, she had entirely become the Princess they all desired her to be. The soul of the Princess was there, in this painting of the odd girl with the dark skin and the strange hair curling out from under her turban. Princess Caraboo. Mrs Worrall would have her proof that the Princess had existed, and suffer no misfortune from any kind of hurtful or uncomfortable gossip. She would not have her possessions stolen by Captain Palmer, or her family's name dragged through the mud.

All her memories would be preserved in this picture.

Looking at it, Princess Caraboo knew that she was now free to be someone else. She could have danced there and then.

Outside, through the door that led out into the artist's garden, she could see that the sun was shining. The artist's pocket watch told her it was nearly twelve. She climbed back into her chair. The man was bound to break for lunch, wasn't he? By that time the captain would have found a local hostelry and would be working his way to the bottom of a glass, and she would be making her way into the centre of town. She would take the fabric the artist had draped around her shoulders as a cloak, leaving him her turban in exchange. She would dance out of Bristol, and if she could earn a little money, maybe there was an alternative to taking the stage to Exeter. This was Bristol. The harbour was crammed with ships going everywhere, anywhere, all across the world. Anywhere.

She felt sure the painting was some kind of sign. She would miss Mrs Worrall's kindnesses, and Cassandra too, and, though she would have laughed at the thought only a week ago, she would miss Fred. But they would not be interested in her any more – Caraboo was there, in the picture, for them to keep for ever.

She felt brave again.

*

It was neither Princess Caraboo nor Mary Willcox who left Mr Barker's studio on the premise of relieving herself in the privy. It was a girl without a name – she'd find one soon enough – wrapped in what could have been a kind of toga, her hair stuffed into a boy's flat cap which she'd found in the hall.

A few boys playing on the road called out as she passed, but she paid them no mind at all. She ran, her bare feet slapping hard on the flat road, all the way back into town, past the great open earthworks that were the new docks, heading for the quayside, where the huge ships packed the river's edge like a wooden city. There were so many people – none, admittedly, as outlandishly dressed as herself, but several not far off. There was the smell of tobacco and spices, and things she didn't even have names for.

She breathed in deep and tasted the salt, and carried on down the hill. She made it all the way to a vantage point on a street than ran above the dockside, where she leaned on a rail and watched the ships, ignoring the shouts, stares and whoops of passers-by and stevedores. There were all sorts of people: lascars, even browner than Caraboo, white-turbaned, lugging sacks off a huge four-master; another boat was crewed by Greeks or Turks, she thought. And Africans, Americans, and some

West Country men – she could tell by their speech. So much activity!

The sun shone down on her as if blessing her new enterprise, and she decided that she would choose a new name better than Mary, which was two or three a penny. The ships all had grand names – *Enterprise* and *Venturer* – she'd had enough of that sort of name. The family next door in London, the Silvers, had all had beautiful names; that was why she had chosen Solomon for her baby. The girls were called Esther and Ruth. Good names both, but she decided on Ruth: it sounded like a soft breath out, and it rhymed with truth. That's who she would be, hard-working, honest Ruth. Ruth would need clothes – a plain skirt, dark material preferably, not too showy, and a white apron. If she could knock on a few doors, offer to clean – anything – just enough for a pair of boots and a second-hand dress, then perhaps she could find a passenger ship that was taking settlers somewhere new – America . . .

All at once, even without the modest clothes she knew Ruth would favour, the world seemed all possibilities, all new. She hadn't felt so happy in a long time.

Suddenly, from a tavern down below on the dockside, she heard a shout. It was only men fighting. Ruth pulled her cap lower over her face. She must go away from here, perhaps find a church or a synagogue. She reminded herself that just because she felt brave, she was not necessarily safe.

She had turned to climb back up to town when she heard a loud crack, bone against stone. She looked back at the fight and realized that it wasn't a fight at all. Three sailors – two as tall as they were wide, a third smaller – were setting about one well-dressed unfortunate. When they were certain that he was insensible, they pulled off his jacket, his boots and his pocket watch. Ruth saw that he was fair-haired, and even from this distance noticed the dark red blood spreading from a cut on his head.

When Fred walked into the Maiden's Farewell he knew that he might well be on the right track. At the Admiralty there had been no record of a Captain Palmer of the right age. He'd been directed to the Maiden's Farewell because, the clerk assured him, the landlord, Mr Hurst, had been a sailor, and knew everything there was to know about the South Seas, having spent his life on East Indiamen sailing as far east as Peking.

It had not occurred to Fred to feel afraid until he walked through the door. In London he had entered many such low dives, but always mob handed – Edmund and fellows from school; they would drink the low beer and laugh at the poor sort, and return to their school and their warm beds and their money.

Fred thought it best to show no fear. If he did, no doubt this pack of press gang rejects – which is what at a glance the drinkers looked like – would fall upon him.

It was dark and his head almost brushed the low ceiling; he smelled stale beer, wood smoke, tobacco and sweat. He kept walking until he reached the bar counter, aware of three men hunched over a table playing dominoes, another knot playing cards. Fred knew he must not, on any account, look indecisive or weak. He was aware that every eye was on him; he was also aware that the value of his jacket alone was probably equal to the combined cost of every scrap and thread of clothing in the whole place.

Fred ordered a beer and attempted to pay using the smallest coin he could lay his hand on. He cursed under his breath – why hadn't he thought first and then acted!

The man behind the bar did not look as old as Captain Palmer, but his face was weather-beaten and leathery like his. His arms were covered in dark blue tattoos, the like of which Fred had never seen, not even in London – not the usual sailors' mottoes, or anchors or flowers, but strange whorls and curlicues.

'South Seas,' the man said. 'Put your eyeballs back in your head, lad.'

'Oh, yes, right.'

As Fred took the tankard of dubious, cloudy ale,

he knew that the whole bar was listening. He looked at the innkeeper: this was the man he needed to talk to. 'Mr Hurst?'

'Mebbe. Who's asking?'

Fred took a sip of the sour beer. Perhaps he would have done better to stick to spirits, he reflected. He lowered his voice. 'My name is Worrall.' He tried to sound firm. 'I'm looking for Captain Palmer. Served in Malay, Indian Ocean.'

Mr Hurst looked at him. Fred noticed that where one eye was blue, the other was milky white and clouded. 'Palmer?' He spat onto the floor.

Fred took another sip. 'Did you sail with him? Know of him? In Java? Sumatra? Tells a lot of tales – Penanggalan, bloodsuckers . . .'

One of the company laughed. 'The only bloodsuckers round here are the rich!'

The innkeeper stared at Fred with his good eye. 'What's it worth to you?'

'Two guineas.' Fred hoped his face was stony as he set the money down on the bar.

Mr Hurst raised his eyebrows and, apparently satisfied, leaned forward. 'Aye, I know a Palmer,' he said. 'Been in here more'n once, collecting stories. I tell you what, though. I've spent the past twenty years crisscrossing the Indian Ocean like it was the Corn Market, and I never heard nor seen nothing of any Captain Palmer until he walked through the door of my inn.'

'You're sure? He said he was in Sumatra – for five years, round about the turn of the century . . . did a lot of business . . .'

The innkeeper shook his head. 'I tell you, lad, I know your man, and he likes to spin tales all right, but mark me, that cove's seen more rum in his life than seawater, and I wouldn't trust him as far as I could throw him. I could tell you things about that man . . .' He shook his head, and spat on the floor again.

'Yes?' Fred leaned forward, but the innkeeper just laughed and swept the two guineas off the counter into his hand. Fred knew what that meant. He'd have to pay up if he wanted to know more.

He put his tankard down on the counter. 'I've heard all I need to, thank you.'

Caraboo had been right, then. Palmer was crooked. And knowing that, he could threaten the man, force him to leave . . .

A chill thought struck him. If Palmer was a fake, if he had never been to the South Seas, what was that dialect he spoke with the Princess? And what was she?

He pushed the thought away. Perhaps he had picked it up in places like the Maiden's Farewell, along with his ghost stories . . . Perhaps.

Fred got up, and the company went back to their games. Maybe he had been foolish to see the place as a den of thieves ready to fall upon him for whatever he had in his pocket. The clock behind the bar chimed two o'clock; he was late for his meeting with Mama and Cassandra.

He stepped out into the street. Mama would not be pleased to learn that the captain was a fraud, but if he was threatening Caraboo—

'Watch where you're going!' A huge man barged into him and almost knocked him to the ground.

'I say!' Fred exclaimed back, and the second he said it he knew it was a mistake. He felt the blow across the back of his legs that felled him, and cried out as his head cracked on the stone pavement, and the whole world went black.

For a moment the world slowed for Ruth. She told herself she had never seen that man before in her short life. She was brand new, unburdened.

But now the blood had spread out in a small circle, like a halo around his blond head. A hundred souls walked past, a boy only stopping to check his breeches pocket for change. No one was doing anything!

Ruth gathered her toga tight around her and ran.

When she reached the man, she sat down, cradling his head, unwound the toga and used it to staunch the flow of blood.

'Someone fetch a doctor!' she yelled, as fiercely as she could. 'NOW!'

10

TRUE DECEIVERS

The Maiden's Farewell
Bristol
June 1819

Frederick Worrall was laid out on a table in the back
bar of the Maiden's Farewell. The bleeding had stopped,
and although Fred was out cold, the sawbones who'd
been called down off an ocean-going four-master looked
him over and pronounced him alive.

'Are you sure, sir?' the girl said. She was still trembling a little.

The doctor pulled back Fred's eyelids, and then
leaned close. 'As I can be. There's breath here, see.' He
gestured towards Fred's mouth. 'The blood's all show.
This one's a long way from death.' He shouted at the
innkeeper, 'Fetch us a pitcher of your finest Adam's ale
and I'll show you a modern Lazarus come to Bristol

dockside!' He laughed and clapped his hands together.

The girl watched as the doctor took the jug and threw it over Fred Worrall, and in seconds he came coughing and spluttering to life; sitting up, just as she imagined Lazarus in the Bible, white-faced and still smeared with blood. The doctor thumped him heartily on the back and handed him a tot of brandy. Fred coughed as it went down, but it seemed to spark him into life somehow.

The girl showed two emotions on her face: relief and fear. She turned away from the young man and followed the doctor to the door.

'There you are, little lady,' the doctor said as he left. 'Job done. Tell your young master to leave me three shillings' worth of rum on account with the innkeeper – for Doctor Bernard of the *Robert and Anne* – and I'll be one happy soul.'

The girl nodded, her voice low. 'He is not my master. He is Mr Worrall; his father owns the Tolzey Bank – he'll see you right, I am sure. Thank you, sir.'

She stopped. One second too long – a last look back at the man on the table.

Fred looked around the room, rubbing his temple, where the blood was now congealing and a great egg-shaped lump had grown. 'Where in God's own name am I?' He looked at the girl by the door, staring hard, his mind as woolly as one who'd drunk three skins full.

Fred screwed up his face. The light was behind her, but the girl was definitely wearing Caraboo's toga. However, she had no turban, but wore a boy's cap. He struggled to concentrate . . . The voice that had come from her mouth, the voice that he had heard, and not in his dreams, surely belonged to somebody else. His head throbbed. Perhaps he was still, in some kind of fashion, unconscious.

'Who the hell are you?' he said.

The girl stood there, frozen. She should have run then. Run as fast as she could. Instead she was transfixed. A rabbit glaring at a lamp, awaiting the bullet.

She didn't know what to say. The Princess Caraboo no longer existed, except in oils – although she had to admit she was still wearing her clothes, holding a knife. She shut her eyes. The relief she'd felt when she heard that Frederick Worrall hadn't died, along with the dread that the future was about to spiral out of control, made her nauseous.

'Hey! Sir! I say!' Fred called after the doctor and tried to stand up, steadying himself against the table. But the doctor had gone and Fred was still too befuddled to support himself, so he slid into a seat Mr Hurst offered.

'Caraboo? You are covered in . . .' Fred looked at his own hands, his shirt front. 'This is my blood? Oh God . . .'

'Mostly water, sir,' the innkeeper said. 'The strange maid here did well by you; you owe her your life.' He looked from the girl to Fred and back. 'I'll get my lad to fetch you a cab to take you home. Your people can pay if you don't have the coin at present.'

'I'm best leaving, sir,' the girl said quietly. She stood up, eyes fixed on the ground.

'What? What did you say? *Go?* No you don't!' Fred half lunged after her, caught her by the arm, and she tried to pull away. 'You! Speak! Who – what – are you?'

'Please, sir, will you let me go?' Her voice belonged to someone else completely – a soft West Country burr that spoke of buttermilk and pastures.

Fred shook his head. 'Not till you look me in the eye, dammit!'

The girl could feel his hand tight around her forearm. The blood was rushing to her cheeks. She thought she might faint clear away, and wouldn't that be a blessing? She closed her eyes for a moment, but he was still there, his hand like a vice around her arm.

She had the knife in her belt: she could slash him with it, she thought, draw a bigger cut across his pretty face and see him blinded with blood, then run out through the kitchen and away. But not in real life; not hurt someone she knew. She crumpled. All the fight had left her.

'You leave the girl be, I say!' said Mr Hurst. 'She saved you – whether or not you'd die, or whether suffer more blows from the mob, who knows? Either way, you owe her.' He turned to Caraboo. 'I won't be a minute. Do you trust yourself with him? I do believe his brain is yet addled.'

She swallowed. She wanted to follow the innkeeper out of the room and get herself as far away from Fred Worrall as possible. 'I must go also,' she said, but Fred threw himself against the door.

'No! You will talk to me – for heaven's sake, talk!'

He looked at her: he was so confused – she could see it in his eyes, and she felt a little sorry for him. Her mind was racing. What could she say?

'You are not Caraboo?' Fred's voice was low, and he was shaking. 'Our Princess Caraboo? You spoke! I do not understand. I heard you . . . with another's voice! I swear it!'

She shook her head.

'What are you then?'

'Only a girl.'

'There it is!' Fred laughed. 'That voice! That damned *English* voice!'

Her heart was beating triple time, her eyes were round; once again she looked like a rabbit caught in lamplight.

'Liar! Damned liar!'

The girl moved back, pressed herself against the wall.

'It was you,' Fred said. 'You and that bloody captain. Plotting together, the pair of you! You had us all hooked. I was hooked – a soft-hearted fool, believing you were real! Those days on the island, were they all sham?'

'No!'

'I cared . . .' Fred looked away. 'You, a princess! Hah!'

'It wasn't like that, sir!'

He jabbed a pointing finger at her. 'Oh, it was exactly like that! I was right all along. Laughing at me, at us, were you? Do you know what you have done to my family?'

'I meant to go.' Her voice was soft. 'I didn't mean to stay. The captain made me, sir.' She was shaking. 'I should never have stayed.'

'Witch! Don't act the innocent! Oh, I was right all along! You knew what you were doing, you were a flatty catcher, a thief, a swindler. I shall turn you over to the magistrates. I shall do it today! To think that I was taken in by you . . .' He shouted for the innkeeper. 'Sir! Landlord! Fetch me the constables! Call out the militia!'

The girl shook her head. 'Please, sir, no, sir – you must believe me!'

'*Must believe you?*' He frowned. 'You and that Captain

Palmer have dragged the Worralls through the filth!'

'No! I never heard of him before I arrived at Knole! I only went along with him, until—'

'Went along with him!' Fred was speechless for a moment. 'You led us all a dance.'

'I am sorry, sir.'

'Sorry! I will make sure you pay . . .'

'If this goes to court, won't it be even worse for your family, for your mother?'

'Why would you care?'

'Mrs Worrall was only kindness, sir!'

'And you made a fool of her!'

'It was never meant so, sir!'

Fred slid to the floor, back against the door.

'Are you well, sir? You have lost a deal of blood.'

'You may as well have done this yourself with your knife, lady – no, I say the wound you made is a deal deeper.'

She said nothing. Hadn't she wanted him weak like this – bootless, jacketless, with nothing, like this? She closed her eyes. She had not thought . . .

'I never meant this.' She shuddered, holding back the tears. 'God will judge me, sir.'

'And the City of Bristol magistrates too.' Fred tried to sit up. 'Pass me that water,' he said.

She nodded. She could see the vein in his neck

pulsing. She took a deep breath and tried to talk softly. 'You must not overreach yourself, sir, or the cut will open again.'

There was a banging on the door behind Fred. Mr Hurst shouted, 'Is all well?'

Fred shouted back that it was, and that he was to send a man to fetch the constables.

The girl shook her head. 'Please, no!' she whispered.

'Are you certain?' came the innkeeper's voice.

Fred looked at her: her was face pleading with him. 'Certain!' he answered. 'This girl is a criminal, a liar and a damned thief!'

'I have stolen nothing,' she said.

'You have stolen our family's good name!'

The girl was close to tears.

'For heaven's sake, keep your tears to yourself! I do not care for them.' Fred shifted against the door.

'No, nor do I.' She sniffed.

'So who are you, then? Some brown girl off the ships? Some whore's child brought up to lying and cheating?'

'I was never a cheat!'

'And how do you square that exactly?'

'I believed it. I *was* Caraboo. I was only what your people wanted me to be, nothing more. And I never took a thing that belonged to your family. I suffered Heyford and his electricity, I was discussed and—'

'Oh, so you loved the attention, then?'

The girl thought for a long moment. She looked down at her bare feet. 'I suppose that would be it, sir, yes.' She paused, and then her voice grew calmer. 'And to be something other than who I was; something fresh, something good, something capable of love and being loved.'

'Love?'

'Aren't we all liars when it comes to love?'

'You are mistaken, whatever your name is,' he said hastily. 'Love is honest and true; love does not lie.'

She shook her head. 'I don't believe that.'

'Believe what you like. I am a gentleman.'

'Yes, now, that is a truth of sorts.'

'Of sorts?'

'Have you always acted as a gentleman, sir? At all times?'

'You have no right to talk to me like that!'

'So you have always told the truth to those who would love you?'

'Shut up!' Fred glared. 'All that time, all that time I spoke freely and thought you dumb!'

'Well, I am not. You have no idea about my life, about what it was like, sir.'

'No, and I do not care for more lies.'

'No, sir.'

Outside on the quayside, life went on: the sound of carts trundling over cobbles, of shouts, of men at work. Inside, the light came through the old windows in yellow bars.

'I suppose, if anything, I have been guilty of thinking of nothing, these past weeks at Knole. Caraboo was a princess. She thought nothing of the future but only of the present, of comfort.' She sighed. 'I thought of not wanting to go back to living on the road, and being vulnerable—'

Now he smiled. 'Hah! Vulnerable? You are the fiercest girl I ever met.'

'That was Caraboo,' she said.

'You are Caraboo.'

She shook her head and took a deep breath; took off the cap, and pushed her hand through her dark hair. She could not be Caraboo any more, and she would never be Ruth now.

She looked at him. 'No, sir, I am Mary Willcox, of Witheridge in Devon, just beyond the city of Exeter. I was a nursemaid in London for a year since—'

'Well, Mary, you can keep your tales. Although perhaps the judge and the newspapers will want to talk to you.'

'No! Can't you see that will only make things worse?! If you want to do right by the Worralls, by your mother, we will have to find another way!'

'We?' Fred shook his head. 'What, you would have me let you go? I suppose I must look like an idiot to you, but I assure you I am not.'

'Do you want your family in the papers?'

'No!'

'Then think, sir, I beg you! Your father's business as a banker is built on trust. At the very least he would be laughed at—'

'You could ruin us!' The thought struck Fred, and suddenly his mind raced to a future where the Worralls were the butt of an enormous joke.

'I never meant to . . .'

He wanted to pick her up and shake her. Mother would be heartbroken, and Cass too, but the business? If no one trusted father's judgement because of this stupidity, the bank would go under; the Worralls would not only be a laughing stock, they would be ruined.

'Was Heyford in on it? Or was it just you and Palmer?' Was there anyone he could trust? he wondered.

'No. The captain embroidered my own history, such as it was, sir. I do believe he has his own enrichment in mind – I want nothing to do with the man. He is the one you have to watch, sir.'

'I think you might be out to save your own skin.'

'It is not worth saving, sir.'

'That is the truth!' He cursed, words she hadn't heard before, spitting them out like bullets. 'You know the worst thing of all? I believed you! The tears, the persecution by the captain! You were acting then, no doubt, in order to engage my affections!' He looked her up and down as if she were a piece of meat. 'Women . . . I am a fool! I should have let him have you.'

'I was glad, sir, for your intervention. Believe me, I would have left Knole if he—' She stopped herself. Sighed deeply. That was not quite the truth. 'I stayed for other reasons, but he had a hold on me – he threatened me, you know that.'

'Poor you.'

'You do not understand!'

'You have no cause to get angry. You are no more than a liar and an opportunist; a common thief of trust that hurts and ruins all and everything.'

'And you have never hurt a soul? We are all liars, sir! All of us. One way or another.'

'Not like this,' he said, and they looked at each other for a moment. 'Not like this at all . . .'

They sat in silence for what seemed like an age. She wondered how her life would go from here, and saw no joy.

'Perhaps I took things too far. Yes, I know I did. And I am sorry, again, sir. Mrs Worrall was kind.'

'And you repay her like this! I care only for my mother's good name.'

She leaned forward. 'Your mother should be protected – but, sir, can't you see, handing me over to the constables—'

There was a loud knock on the door. Fred moved aside and let Mr Hurst in. He was followed by two of the Port Authority constables, dressed in a sober livery, truncheons as thick as a man's arm swinging from their belts.

'My good man,' Fred said, getting up and rubbing his sore head, 'I am sorry to have troubled you – the blow to my head—'

'Didn't I say?' the innkeeper replied.

'Yes, I should have paid more attention. I am Frederick Worrall, of Knole Park. My father, Samuel Worrall Esquire, owns the Tolzey Bank.' At this, the constables stood up straighter. Fred went on, 'But I have lost my boots, coat, pocket watch, and been assaulted in the street.'

'This girl any part of it, then?' one of the constables asked.

'No,' Fred said, and he took her hand. 'She is with me.' He looked at her as if she were some piece of trash that had attached itself to his foot. 'She saved my life.' He coughed. 'She was' – he paused – 'set upon also.

We need to return to Knole Park.' He tightened his grip. 'At once.'

Fred did not let go of her hand, even after the constables had left; he led her out into the street and began to march her back up towards the livery stables where he had left his mare. He sent a messenger to the bank, telling his mother not to wait, or worry – something had occurred and he was returning to Knole Park early.

'You are not getting away' – his voice was firm and even – 'Miss Whoever-you-are. You are coming back to Knole Park with me. You will be Caraboo.' She opened her mouth to speak, but he silenced her. 'I say you will! You will keep your mouth shut. You will do your ridiculous dances and talk in your ridiculous cant – at least until Mama's party is over. Then you will disappear and it will be as if you never existed, ever. Do you understand?'

She rode back to Knole Park sitting up in front of him on the mare, his left arm clamped tight about her waist, as if she might float away. She had wriggled at first, but that made him clutch her even more tightly. Her bare legs chafed against the horse, but she knew there was no merit in complaining.

'I had thought to make you walk behind me,' he said, 'but that way we would have taken all afternoon.'

'I shall run away,' she said. 'I ran from the captain,

I shall run from you. You cannot force me to be something against my will!'

'Watch me,' he said, talking to the back of her head. 'If you bolt, I shall say that you have stolen something precious – jewellery, silver. No one would believe you, a lying, worthless milkmaid, over me. I shall drop you in it so deep that hanging will seem like a mercy.'

'I have been to hell, sir, more than once.'

'Then I shall make certain the gates are shut tight for good, the next time.'

11

A Princess Returns

Knole Park House
June 1819

On her return to Knole Park, Cassandra was not in an agreeable mood. The trip to the milliner's had not yielded anything close to her idea of the perfect summer bonnet, and then something had happened to Fred, and Mama threw over all their shopping plans to hurry back home without a detour to the better draper's to buy some new ribbon for her dress.

Diana would be arriving tomorrow, and she was bound to have a brand-new dress for the summer; Cassandra had only the dress from the New Year's Ball, which she could not possibly wear again, and her good summer Indian cotton, which without some new blue ribbon – she had imagined the ensemble, and the ribbon would have been just the thing – would be merely tired.

Then, on returning home, she found that Will Jenkins had left a note – a note! – for her at the house. It might look innocent enough to the untrained eye, but if Mama had not been so taken up with the party and with Fred's accident and with Princess Caraboo, she would surely have noticed. Cassandra thanked heaven that she did not – she merely said it was from Diana and tucked it away as quick as a flash.

Cassandra cursed under her breath. She had told him never to leave notes! He really was too forward. How on earth could she ever have imagined running away with him? She blushed at the thought. For several nights she had really entertained the idea of being an innkeeper's wife. Thank God she had never told Diana! She shuddered.

Oh, he was handsome, but far too earnest – he thought of work and money more than was necessary. She sighed. Edmund Gresham would be here tonight, and he was entertaining, witty, and never mentioned anything half so boring as earnings or income.

She cast an eye over the note. It said that she should come to the lakeside: he wanted to meet her today, before the visitors arrived. Cassandra sighed. She would have to go, in case he caused some scene in front of Mama's guests; it would be unbearable. Why could Will Jenkins not take a hint? It was unfair!

She did not want to be cruel, to cast him off. He must know that!

She would have to go and tell him not to bother her any more. That she had made a mistake; that Will was certain to find someone more suitable to his station – no, she would not say that. Someone who could love him better than she – yes, that was it. And then that would be that.

She was about to change out of her town dress when Phoebe came in bearing some of Cook's home-made lemonade.

'Miss Cassandra!' she whispered.

'It is all right, Phoebe,' Cassandra said. 'No one is listening. Did you finish the dress for Princess Caraboo?'

'Yes, miss, but it's your brother, Miss Cassandra. Something terrible—'

'Mama told me he was robbed in the street! In broad daylight! Bristol is not safe.'

'But he was covered in blood!'

'Covered? Mama said he was attacked, knocked down, but that he was all right, thank goodness.'

'Well, perhaps not covered. He's all right, miss, but his jacket is quite ruined. And do you know, miss – Caraboo was covered in blood too?' Phoebe gave Cassandra a look. 'I reckon she was with him.'

'Are you certain, Phoebe? I thought she was at the

artist's with the captain?' She stared at Phoebe, who was grinning.

'That's it, miss – the captain, miss, he's not returned! Mrs Worrall is all of a flutter, in case he's not coming back. I wager the man's had too many spirits, or is in some inn between here and Bristol telling his tales.'

'Well, that's no surprise – but Fred and Caraboo? Together?'

'I know, Miss Cassandra,' Phoebe said. 'And they are both in such low spirits. Heaven knows what happened!'

'I shall make it my mission to discover all, Phoebe. In fact, I will call on Caraboo now. She can accompany me to the lake.'

Cassandra knew that Caraboo might not be able to tell her what happened in so many words, but she was sure she would be able to discover some information. They were both young women, after all, albeit from different continents. And it would make all the difference if she could see Will with Caraboo present. It would put some distance between them; he would not be able to press his suit and she would be much more able to resist.

She walked down to the lake with Cassandra. She was wearing one of Cassandra's cast-offs, cut short for ease of movement. She had Caraboo's old black turban on her head, her knife at her belt, and a bow and arrows slung around her shoulder, but she was not sure if she felt like Caraboo at all. Cassandra ran on ahead and she closed her eyes, feeling the sunlight on her face and the soft grass under her feet. This was, she told herself, a mess entirely of her own making.

'Phoebe tells me that you and Fred returned together! What happened? Was he your brave protector?' Cassandra put her fists up. 'And the captain? Did he fall out with Mr Barker? I can't imagine the two got on.'

Caraboo shrugged.

'Oh, I do so wish you could tell me everything!' said Cassandra. 'Wait till this evening – I have something to show you that will raise your spirits, Princess.'

Caraboo nodded politely, although she thought the one thing she could do without was any kind of surprise.

Then Cassandra forgot about her brother and proceeded to babble on about Will and Ed – which of them was fairest, which was tallest.

The Princess Caraboo ran her hand along the tops of the rushes that bordered the lake.

'I will own that Will is broader about the shoulder, but he has become so tiresome! I had a puppy once – oh, I loved him straight away . . . I think I was nine or ten.' Cassandra pulled a face, remembering. 'I put my Sunday ribbon about his neck and he followed me everywhere.

Then he grew up, and his disposition, I swear, changed from one day to the next. From waiting happily for tit-bits, now he barked and snapped, and snapped some more. Papa was all for drowning the poor animal, but I put my foot down and gave him to the gamekeeper's boy. Never did see the animal again . . .'

The Princess said nothing. She remembered how Fred had spoken to her. That would only be the start, she thought. She would not be interesting, she would be like that puppy; there would be only blows and curses.

Cassandra sighed. 'Your face is so long, Princess, it will sweep the floor. What was it that happened in Bristol?' She cocked her head to one side, in order to express sympathy, and leaned close, expecting some kind of answer.

Caraboo was grateful for the sound of twigs snapping as Will Jenkins, waiting by the lake, stood up sharp when he saw them coming.

'Miss Cassandra!' he said, already sad. 'I thought you would be alone!'

Does he not know, Caraboo thought, *that she no longer wants him?* She looked from one to the other: Cassandra, perfect, smiling, golden; Will Jenkins, his good looks soured by desperation.

Cassandra flapped a hand dismissively. 'Oh, do not worry, we can talk.' She smiled at him. 'She will not know what we are saying. She knows only yes and no and please and thank you.'

It was an education, Caraboo thought, watching the two of them: Cassandra not saying what she needed to say, Will not wanting to recognize it.

He spoke of a passage to America, of savings, and of marriage; Cassandra kept her distance, talking only of how busy she would be, and how she regretted not buying any blue ribbon.

The Princess thought that if she had been Will Jenkins she would have walked away a thousand times; but he wanted her so much – it was written in his every movement. Caraboo looked away. She reminded herself that this was what she had planned for Fred, this devotion, so that she could cast him off and he would know hurt and pain.

It served her right. She should have left weeks ago, after the first night in clean linen. The Worralls did not deserve what she had done to them, even if she had never meant any harm.

She looked away, across the water. Her colour was up – she could feel it in her face – and her head thumped. She was aware of every blood vessel, she thought, as they carried the blood this way and that around her body. Her father would say it was shame she felt, and should feel; barrels of the stuff. Then she remembered the letters. She had to go back to the house, tell Fred at once that his plan was bound to fail, given that in some professor's study in Oxford or Edinburgh, her handwriting was being pored over. Real professors, not fairground showmen with letters after their name, like Heyford. They were bound to see the truth – and who knew, perhaps there were replies on their way to Knole Park at this moment—

'Miss Cassandra, please, when we met before—'

Cassandra looked away.

'When we . . .' Will looked at Caraboo as if embarrassed, and although she willed him not to say any more, he went on, lowering his voice to a whisper. 'We – you – we spoke of running away, of being together, of America. I need to know now, I need to know if you meant it.'

'Oh, Will!' Cassandra smiled at him. 'I cannot speak of this, Caraboo is here!'

'But you said—'

'I know.' She could not meet his gaze. 'But she might get the wrong shape of things.' She touched his arm. 'Will, do not be so tiresome. We have all our lives . . .'

'You promised me,' Will said.

And then the Princess Caraboo was sick in the rushes at the side of the lake. Cassandra, most grateful for the interruption, immediately hurried her away to the house.

*

The Greshams' coach had just pulled up on the drive. Fred watched his mother from the hall and wished she wouldn't fawn so over Lady Gresham. It was more of a relief than he had imagined, seeing Edmund, though.

'My word, Fred, what happened to your face? Have you found a calling as a prize fighter?'

'Alas, no. It is a long story.'

'Well, there'll be plenty of time for the telling, and I shall have no competition for the ladies. Hah!'

'No, Edmund, I am in no position to be sensational like this.'

'Oh! I need a drink. The roads are so hard I thought I might die in there with Mother for three whole hours. Oh God, the countryside is dull! And months before any decent hunting! With any luck I shall be on a boat bound for the Mediterranean before I die of boredom.'

'Think of me, brother, with only dry Classics, and drier old men, to look forward to.'

'I promise I will not. When I set foot in Italy I will think of nothing but my own pleasure!' Edmund said. 'And do you know, you look like a man who has forgotten how to have fun? Is that possible? I had heard this princess of yours was quite fascinating. My mother has spoken of little else since she received the invitation.'

'I suppose she *has* turned the household upside down.' Fred wasn't sure if he could tell Edmund the truth about the Princess just yet.

'And your lovely sister, the beautiful Cassandra – is she still carrying a torch for me?'

'Ed, I have warned you about Cassandra. Just because she throws herself at you . . . You would do well to remember that she is my sister.'

'And I am your friend.'

'And I bested you in three fights at school.'

'She is safe with me! Unless I marry her, of course, but that is a century away at least.'

'Don't let her – or Mama – hear you dangle marriage like that, Ed. She will surely faint with delight.'

Edmund laughed. 'The ladies of Leghorn and Tuscany and Venice are waiting. I don't know if your sister can compete.'

'I *will* knock you down, Edmund.'

'I cower before you, Frederick.'

Fred rolled his eyes. But at least he was smiling.

'And there will be dancing?' Edmund asked.

'Mama has booked musicians from Bath.'

'Thank God! And I have heard' – Edmund lowered his voice as they went inside – 'that your princess is a regular smasher.'

'I assure you she is not *my* princess at all. She's down

by the lake, I think – at least, I saw her heading off there with Cass.'

'Then let us kill two birds with one stone. My refreshment can wait,' Edmund said, marching Fred out onto the terrace and down across the park.

The girls were walking towards them, arm in arm. Fred saw that his sister was talking animatedly about something. The other girl was beside her, her shoulders slumped, her attitude listless; even from a distance she looked sad. Fred would have liked to shake her. What right did she have to be sad? She had promised to play the Princess, and he wanted the running, dancing, fighting one, not a sulky girl. How would Mama feel if the stupid girl let everyone down?

'Edmund, Fred!' Cassandra waved, and as they drew closer Fred saw that Caraboo was quite pale.

'What's happened?'

'Caraboo has been sick, just now, by the lake! Oh, Edmund' – Cassandra blushed – 'you have arrived.'

'Indeed I have.'

'Fred' – she turned to her brother – 'I am taking Caraboo up to the house, to Bridgenorth. I think she is not well. It's such a shame for you, Edmund, to see her like this. I'm afraid she is not herself at all! Come, I am sure you need some refreshments after your long journey.'

Fred stared at Caraboo. The girl was a liar; she could be faking this as surely as she had faked everything else.

'Hello – Princess.' Edmund spoke to her slowly and loudly as if she were a small deaf idiot.

'Edmund, don't be silly – she's no fool,' Cassandra said. She turned to the Princess. 'This is Edmund Gresham.'

'Esquire,' Edmund added, bowing slightly.

The Princess returned a salute – although it was lacklustre, Fred thought, and definitely half-hearted. He bit his tongue.

'I say, Princess,' Edmund said, reaching out to touch her face as if she were a small child, or a dog.

She stepped back.

'She doesn't like being touched. By men,' Cassandra explained.

Edmund looked at Fred and snorted. 'What a poor show! What does she like, then!'

'Don't be so mean, Edmund.' But Cassandra was smiling as she spoke. 'I will take her to her room. I will see you gentlemen at dinner.' And she led the Princess away.

Edmund put his hands in his pockets and turned to Fred. 'I say, did you know that! The touching, I mean?' He cursed. 'And she is a corker. A bit peaky now – vomiting's never a plus in a girl – but a definite looker.

I'd have a crack at her! Fred, I was banking on you having broken the girl in by now! I mean, sir, you are, are you not, Mr Frederick Worrall, a man capable of charming any girl in Westminster into bed . . .'

Fred glared at his friend. It was as if he was looking in a mirror – only somehow time had shifted in the weeks he had been down from school and he knew that wasn't his reflection any more. He turned away. Edmund was talking about something else now, and he was grateful for it. All those girls, all those Lettys and Hettys . . . He had bought those girls' compliance with money, and even then some wept. The society girls who flirted with him didn't know him at all, wanted only a pretty face and some silly soft-soap flattery.

He thought of Caraboo, by the fire on the island. She was the only girl who knew him at all, he thought. And she didn't even exist.

'There!' Cassandra and Phoebe stood back to admire their work. 'I am so glad you recovered, Princess. Mama, as usual, has plans for this evening and tomorrow, and I thought you would need something a little more elegant.'

Caraboo could not help smiling. She had never worn anything that felt so delicious in all her life. It was cream satin that shimmered almost golden as she turned this way and that, looking at herself in the mirror, wishing she truly was a princess who could do as she pleased.

'Oh! You are a picture!' Cassandra said. 'Phoebe, your needle does you credit.'

Phoebe bobbed a curtsey. 'Thank you, miss. I made it from the mistress's old chemise.'

Caraboo saluted her, then kissed her on the cheek. If she could have spoken English she would have thanked them both. The dress came down just below her knees – modest for Caraboo – and was cut square about the neck, like her hunting dress. The sleeves and hem were crenellated, and swished when she moved. Caraboo felt the Princess return a little, and danced around the room; Cassandra joined her.

'Come along, Phoebe!' she said, and the three of them made a wonderful picture. Until Cassandra, out of breath, stopped and leaned against the window.

'There, look! The captain is returned on some kind of wagon!'

Caraboo followed her gaze, and her heart sank. The man was lying spark out on a cart being pulled by a tired old farm horse. The cart stopped and the man slid off and made his way unsteadily into the house.

She looked at herself in the mirror and thought of fairgrounds and punters as drunk as him, prodding her, shouting at her. She was a fraud – not a princess any more, but Mary Willcox dressing up. Her stomach churned.

Cassandra was laughing. 'You know, I never saw a man get so drunk so often and live.'

'You ent seen my father, miss,' Phoebe laughed too.

'Oh, you do look beautiful, Princess.' Cassandra sighed. 'I shall look like a sparrow beside a swan next to you. My only hope is that you do not steal away my Edmund's heart.'

The pretend Princess Caraboo's first thought was that Edmund Gresham didn't have a heart at all. Perhaps a pump to circulate the blood, but nothing tender. He reminded her of the seagulls that preyed on rubbish in town, small beady eyes regarding everything and seeing the value in nothing.

After the party had gone down for dinner, the fake Princess Caraboo sat on the roof, watching the sun set in the west, letting her legs swing free over the parapet of Knole Park. If she were truly Caraboo, she thought, she would not let the captain's threat of fairgrounds – or Fred's of imprisonment – worry her at all. She would merely stand up here in her beautiful silk dress, spread her arms, and fly all the way back to Javasu.

Her heart thumped at the thought of going downstairs, of performing. She had never felt like this before.

Could she do it? Could she be Princess Caraboo again?

She stood up and stepped up onto the parapet. The Princess used to love heights. A breeze came in off the lake and she closed her eyes.

Hell, she thought, was all around her; hell was here. Hell was baby Solomon gone, hell was in a Wiltshire cherry orchard, hell was broken hearts and loving those who never ever loved you back, hell was dancing for crumbs and sleeping in barns. She shut her eyes. She had tried life, she thought, as Mary Willcox, as Princess Caraboo, as farm girl, nursemaid, lover, mother, beggar, actress. She had not been good at any of them. She stepped out, one foot over the void. Perhaps she should show them all that she was not afraid of anything.

12

PRINCESS CARABOO REQUESTS YOUR COMPANY

Knole Park House
June 1819

Fred did not recognize half the staff in the dining room.
Mama had mentioned borrowing the Edgecombes' cook
– she must have half their household here, he thought.
The guests, apart from the professor and the village
parson, the Greshams and the Edgecombes, seemed to
be academics who wore old-fashioned jackets, or thick
glasses, or both, deep in discussion with some of Mama's
friends from her anthropolgical circle. Most argued
about Caraboo, but only a few, he noted, doubted her
veracity.

The professor from Oxford, a collegaue of Heyford's,
was convinced. 'I have seen her writing – she is real!
And I have spent three months in Calcutta . . .'

'Mrs Worrall would not be taken in. She is intelligent – for a woman. And an American.'

Fred studied the man and thought more and more that university would be a waste of his time.

The food was, he had to admit, good, – meat jellies and pies, and even a representation of the island of Javasu worked entirely in coloured sugar paste. But he was not hungry.

He was sitting opposite Edmund and Cassandra. He felt like an old grey-haired cynic watching them flirt and talk so much rubbish. Then Professor Heyford enquired about Edmund's forthcoming tour, and Edmund trotted out his itinerary. Cassandra told them how, thanks to Mrs Shelley's *Frankenstein*, she wished to see the Alps.

Professor Heyford and Edmund laughed.

Cassandra pouted. 'It is not fair! Why may young men travel the world and not young ladies?'

'My dear girl,' Professor Heyford said, 'travel is dangerous, and most uncomfortable – so I've been told.'

'Our princess managed it all the way across the world,' Cassandra said.

'But you are *English*,' Heyford said.

'I am as strong as Caraboo, I'm sure!'

'Oh! You can swim and hunt and climb?' Fred asked her.

'No, but I could if I wanted to,' Cassandra said. 'My skills are—'

Edmund cut in, 'Your skills are being the most perfect adornment to society.'

Cassandra blushed and giggled, and Fred thanked heaven he'd been born a man. What could Cassandra do? If there was anything she wanted for, she had only to ask, to inveigle; she could not possibly step out into the world on her own.

He sighed. Wasn't he following a course set for him by so many others? He smeared his strawberry cream around the plate. Everything was false – not just the Princess, but the whole evening: all these people, smiling but wanting so much from each other. His mother wanting a titled lady like Edmund's mother at her table; his sister wanting Edmund, and Edmund wanting anything but boredom. Professor Heyford was a fool of a different stripe. Was he really taken in by the girl? Or was he only going along with it all so as to have his contributions listened to?

They were all fools and liars just as much as the Princess upstairs. He pushed his plate away.

In the library the chairs had been set out for a lecture. The terrace doors were open behind the curtains as the night was still – even now that it was at last growing dark – too warm. The easel from the schoolroom had been set up and Professor Heyford had pinned up a phrenology chart showing the human head divided into sections, like the counties of some strange skull-shaped country. He busied himself arranging a pointer he had borrowed from Miss Marchbanks, and reading over copious notes under his breath.

Mrs Worrall sidled up to Fred. 'Would you fetch Caraboo down? I think she might be on the roof – Finiefs tells me she isn't in her room. Oh, and I forgot to ask Finiefs if the captain is fit for the lecture – I am certain Lady Gresham would so enjoy his tales of the Penanggalan.'

Fred finished his drink, and as he put the glass down on the table the whole party fell silent and turned towards the terrace windows.

Finiefs opened the doors; outside the sun was low in the sky which had turned a fantastic, dazzling crimson. Fred wanted to turn away – it almost hurt to look.

The buzz of conversation quietened, and there against the blood-red sun he saw the dark silhouette of the Princess Caraboo making her way across the lawn towards the house. One or two of the ladies gasped. Fred, despite himself, couldn't help staring.

She came in barefoot, wearing a dress that shimmered as she moved. She had taken off her turban and wore a kind of wreath made of ivy around her head. She looked straight ahead, but even though she walked as Caraboo had done, she couldn't feel that regal leopard curling itself around her legs; surely someone would see her shaking . . .

'Princess!' Mrs Worrall gazed at her and smiled. 'You look beautiful!' She wiped a tear from her eye, and led her into the room. 'Princess, this is Lady Gresham and her son, Edmund. They have come especially to see you.'

Lady Gresham looked intrigued. 'Mrs Worrall, she is most delightful!'

Mrs Worrall glowed with delight, Caraboo saluted, and Professor Heyford led her over to a chair.

Edmund sat down next to Fred and said quietly, 'I say, her legs!'

'Mrs Worrall,' Lady Gresham asked, 'is satin the costume of choice in the South Seas?'

Professor Heyford coughed and rapped his pointer against the easel. 'Ladies and gentlemen,' he began, 'the Princess Caraboo.'

He began a lengthy discourse on phrenology. Fred saw the Princess twitch. Cassandra was fiddling with a curl of hair.

Edmund leaned close. 'If I'd known your mama had intended a series of lectures, I would have stayed at home.'

Fred looked over at his mother, fanning herself and looking a little agitated.

Professor Heyford's voice droned on. 'And so, you see, in addition to identifying her previously unrecognizable tongue as from Java, I have been able to deduce, from my investigations and the new science of phrenology, that she is without doubt of noble birth.'

There was a rattle as the library doors opened and Captain Palmer, florid-faced but in a clean set of clothes, came in. He looked at Heyford, then walked right in front of him and the Princess and faced the company.

'I know what you ladies and gentleman want – you want a tale told by a teller who knows . . .'

Lady Gresham grimaced; Mrs Worrall looked worried.

Edmund whispered, 'The fellow's half cut!'

'That is his natural state,' Fred told him.

'This is Captain Palmer,' Mrs Worrall said hastily, 'a seaman of renown.'

'I am that, good lady – ten long years in the South Seas, and adjutant to our governor in Sumatra.' He bowed towards Lady Gresham.

Fred had never heard that tale before.

The captain motioned for the Princess to stand up. Heyford, affronted, protested feebly, but no one took any notice.

'She's lovely, isn't she?' the captain said, sitting in the chair she'd left. 'Though, to be fair, the Malays are without doubt a most attractive, most friendly people.'

Lady Gresham sat up. 'So you speak her language, do you?'

'I do.'

'So who are her people, exactly?'

'Ah, the Princess's father is Jesse Mandu, originally from Congee – what we would call China. According to the Princess, he rules the southern tip of her island home, Javasu.'

He looked at Caraboo and she nodded. 'Javasu.'

'Excuse me, sir,' Edmund leaned forward. 'What I fail to understand,' he drawled, 'is why, if her father is a Chinese, your Princess Caraboo has so little of the Chinese about her – especially the eyes, don't you know.'

There was a ripple of agreement.

'Ahh!' the captain said, and swept his pointer round until it almost touched the Princess. 'You see her skin colour . . .'

'Well, that's it, Captain,' Edmund said. 'To my mind she doesn't look far from an octaroon or some such as you see in town.'

'That's it! That is right on the nose, young man! She is of mixed parentage. In Malay, the races of clear one half of the world swirl and mingle. The people there are all shades of brown and yellow. The Princess's mother, who sadly died many years ago, was a Malay.'

'So she is a mongrel of sorts?' Edmund looked Caraboo up and down.

'Oh, I wouldn't put it like that myself.' The captain stared back at him. 'Princess Caraboo's story is a sad, tragic one. One morning, after prayers, she was walking by the shore outside her palace with her handmaids – three or four of them . . .' He turned to Caraboo, showing three, then four fingers. '*Trua, ne tan?*' he said.

'*Trua,*' she replied, holding up three fingers.

'Three . . . and a pirate ship anchored offshore swooped down upon the helpless maidens and carried them off' – he snapped his fingers – 'just like that! The handmaids were killed instantly – decapitated by sabres, one, two, three!' The captain made hacking motions with his hand, and Cassandra gasped and reached for Edmund's hand for reassurance.

'The sea around the ship foamed red with the young girls' blood. But those fiends saw that Caraboo was worth a small fortune in ransom, so they locked up her below decks. All the while she was crying out for her father—'

'And the pirate ship bought her to England?' Lady Gresham asked.

'Not quite. She was sold for a sack of gold dust to a pirate chief.' The captain sat back in his chair as if exhausted.

Mrs Worrall began applauding. 'Most informative, Captain Palmer. I hope we will hear more about the Princess tomorrow, when Mr Gutch from the *Bristol Advertiser* and Mr Williamson of the Bath Scientific and Literary Society will be joining us. Princess, perhaps you would dance?' She said the word again, louder and slower: 'Dance?'

The Princess saluted Mrs Worrall and moved towards the centre of the room. She had failed to step out into nothing. She was a coward – she did not want to die.

She would do her best to give them Caraboo, she thought, even though her heart was beating so fast it felt as if it might burst. It must be plain as day that she was not a princess; that she was nothing. She stepped right then left, her dress shimmering. A little of the old confidence came back as she danced. She would try her best to be a South Seas princess.

It was a vicious, angry dance. She used the knife, and imagined all her trials and obstacles slashed to pieces. Then, as suddenly as she had begun, she stopped, saluted, and ran out into the dark, her heart thumping. She might have fooled them for now, but it was Mary Willcox who would pay for this. Somehow.

'That was quite remarkable!' Lady Gresham's booming voice was clear even from the terrace.

Princess Caraboo had done her job.

Cassandra slept lightly. Edmund had come close to . . . had almost – she was certain – kissed her. And the night was so warm she tossed and turned, winding herself up in her sheet. She dreamed she was standing at the top of the most famous glacier, the *Mer de Glace*, in Switzerland, wearing some suitably fetching ensemble edged with fur, Edmund Gresham holding her close as the moonlight seared blue across the huge moving river of ice. The sound was of the ground, the ice, creaking and moving under their feet.

'See,' Edmund Gresham said, his eyes dark brown like warm chocolate. 'We can do anything!' She smiled at him, before she realized there was another figure standing a little way off. She could smell him in the cold crisp air. It was Will Jenkins, stripped to the waist and throwing barrels of ale at them, yelling at the top of his voice that Cassandra was his.

She felt the ice move, and her whole body seemed to spin out of control; as she fell, she heard a strange hard noise and her eyes snapped open.

She was in bed – her own bed – with the curtains open and the moonlight streaming in, the light silver and icy, like the Switzerland in her dreams. She gripped the blankets.

The noise came again. Now that she was properly awake, it didn't sound like ice creaking, but was it rain? It couldn't be. The sky was clear.

There! The noise. It wasn't rain, it was gravel thrown up at the window. A parcel of fear unfolded inside her. Frankenstein's monster, she was sure, was standing outside in the park throwing stones up at her window.

Then another sound. Her name, whispered, but loud. 'Miss Cassandra!' More stones.

Whoever it was, it was not a character from a novel made flesh. She pulled on her dressing gown and went to the window.

It was Will Jenkins. He had walked right out of her dream and was standing under her window.

'Miss Cassandra!' He sounded desperate.

'What are you doing?! Anyone could hear!' Cassandra spoke in a stage whisper.

'I need to see you! I've come to the house but you're not—'

'*Shhh!*' She tied the dressing gown tight. 'Come back in the morning!'

'This cannot wait!'

'Are you drunk?'

'No! I have to speak to you!'

Cassandra's heart was thumping at least as loud as Will Jenkins's shouting. If she was not careful, the whole household would be roused and all would be lost.

'I will come down. Wait for me on the terrace!'

Cassandra felt sick. She'd hoped he had understood, after their meeting this afternoon, that things had changed. She could taste something that she imagined must be guilt, sharp and acid at the back of her mouth.

Will Jenkins was not like her, not really, not deep down. He'd never even heard of Mary Shelley. She imagined the look on Mama's face if she knew about their – what was a suitable word? – their *connection*. Which was definitely over. The guilt evaporated. She *had* to do this. For her own sake and her family's.

She took a deep breath and wriggled her feet into her slippers. She had to tell him plainly now; there must be no scene, and this madness would be forgotten. He was not the kind to blab to Father or Mother, was he? No, surely Will Jenkins wouldn't do that. And anyway, who would believe the word of an innkeeper's boy over hers? She felt sick. Believed or not, it could cause no end of damage.

She would give him money if she had to. That pearl necklace she got for her birthday last year had to be worth something.

Cassandra made her way through the silent house

and down the stairs. She tried to breathe deeply and rehearse what she was going to say. She would be kind, she would be firm, she would explain; and he would leave, saddened, but accepting. He must have known it all along. As if someone like him could ever really have a girl like her.

As she crossed the hall, she mouthed every oath she knew, and prayed that God would please make Will Jenkins vanish most completely.

He was sitting on the low wall outside the drawing room, the moonlight across his face. He stood up when he saw her coming, his face softening into a broad smile, and Cassandra felt a pang of something – fancy, perhaps – remembering his kisses . . . But she knew she must be severe.

'Will.'

'Miss Cassandra! Thank heavens!' He took her hands and she pulled them away, pretending to rearrange her dressing gown, then folding her arms tight across herself.

'I had to see you . . . alone. We must make plans – to be together.'

She cleared her throat: the quicker the better, like Vaughan dispatching a lame horse with one blow. It would be for the best. She took a deep breath.

But Will was still speaking. 'America, remember?'

He stared at her intently and Cassandra had to look away. This was too painful.

'Cassandra, please!' He was pleading now. 'You swore love to me, as clear as I stand here—'

'Will, stop it!' she said. 'You are mistaken.'

'Our plans! You said you desired . . .' His voice was a thin croak, and his eyes shone in the moonlight. Was he crying? She had never seen a grown man shed tears.

'Oh, Will! I could never have come away with you! It was a dream, a fancy—'

'Not to me.' He took a deep breath. 'Cassandra, I thought you . . . we . . . I thought there was love . . . you said . . . But you were merely playing with me!' There were no tears now, and the fury in his voice made her back away.

'You should not have come!' she said. 'It was over – the fancy. Do you understand?! And if you tell a living soul about what passed between us, I will deny every word. Every single word!'

She ran back into the house, her eyes blurred with tears. She felt a sickness rising up as she shut her bedroom door behind her. She lay in bed, but managed not a single wink of sleep till dawn. At least, she told herself, she hadn't had to part with the pearls.

*

From her vantage point up on the roof, the Princess Caraboo watched Will stride furiously away.

She had escaped there rather than spend the night in her room, where anyone might find her. She knew the captain wanted words, but she had avoided him, and he had polished off another decanter of Mr Worrall's rum as he told Lady Gresham all about bloodsucking Malaysian spirits.

Poor William Jenkins, he did not deserve to be treated so, she thought as she watched him head out across the moonlit park. It had been like watching a play, hardly real. And she felt guilty for encouraging their affair . . . Something she had thought might be diverting had ended badly. She sighed and rolled herself up in the blanket she had bought from her bedroom.

She watched Will Jenkins make for the village, then change his mind and walk round to the stables. He made an awful noise, a clatter of bolts and doors – it was a miracle that no one stirred, she thought; then, minutes later, she saw him lead Zephyr away from the stables, mount up, and ride off towards Bristol.

What would happen tomorrow? she wondered. She tried to think of nothing and concentrate on counting the stars, which peppered the sky as if someone had been making bread and spilled flour. There were too many.

Lady Gresham had been charmed by Caraboo, and

she had surprised herself. She still enjoyed stepping into the princess's skin, but it was different this time; as if, somehow, Mary Willcox was there at the same time, watching Caraboo dance or salute. The newspaper journalist who was arriving tomorrow afternoon would want her to be real. And the man from the scientific society – would he believe in her?

She counted up to thirty stars, then lost her place and was going to start again, but instead cursed, and shut her eyes. She was utterly alone. And perhaps as long as she was someone else, she always would be.

Caraboo had grown from all those stories she had made up, told first to Peg, then to the children she cared for in London, then whispered to her unborn baby.

Stories had been so much easier than real life. Her own real life, from nursemaid to unwed mother to beggar, reliant on the gifts and kindness of strangers. That was it, she told herself; that was the answer.

No more begging, no more playing. Whatever it cost.

'I am Mary Willcox,' she said aloud to the stars, 'of Witheridge, near Exeter, in Devon.'

13

WHITSUNTIDE

Knole Park House
May, 1819

Mary Willcox had risen early, even before Phoebe. The
roof was hard and the morning dew had chilled her. She
went down to the laundry room and found the dress
she had arrived in, all those weeks ago. It was even
plainer than she remembered, made of dull black stuff
of poor quality, with a high neck and short sleeves.
Wearing this, without a turban, she would be entirely
unremarkable. She put it on and found it far more
restricting than any of Caraboo's clothes. It would be
difficult to climb, to run.

She slipped out of the back door across the morning
fields.

She had barely reached the limit of the park when she
heard the sound of hooves behind her. She turned and

saw Fred Worrall thundering after her on his bay mare.

'Caraboo, come back!' he shouted.

She stopped and faced him, one hand over her eyes, as the sun was already strong. 'I am not Caraboo, sir, as well you know,' she said. 'I am Mary Willcox.'

He looked down at her, and cursed. 'Then, Mary, stop this at once. You promised me Caraboo.'

'I cannot do it, sir.' She shook her head. 'Won't the truth be better?'

'For heaven's sake, what is this longing for the truth? The truth, as you know full well, is never better; it is nastier, it is uglier, rarely better. You had no need of it before, and if you—'

'I am truly sorry.'

'Are you?'

She nodded.

'Then come back to Knole now, if you want to redeem yourself.'

'Sir, whatever you think, when I played Caraboo before, I *believed* it, I wanted desperately to be her. Last night I thought, sometimes, I was myself. It is over. I am done with it.'

'You had them all last night. I cannot let you go.'

'You will force me then, sir?'

'If you look to your conscience, you know that I am right.' He spoke firmly. 'One more day.'

She nodded. What could she do?

Fred jumped down off his horse and made to take her arm; she flinched and moved away.

'I will not run,' she said.

'You promised me that once already.' He grabbed hold of her arm.

'Did I? Did I say "I promise", sir?'

'Does that make the difference?'

'I don't know,' she said.

'I am not used to your voice. It is alien – it does not match your face.'

'My voice! I assure you, sir, it is genuine. My face, though, could belong to anyone.'

'Are you an octaroon, then, as Edmund suggested?'

Mary Willcox shrugged. 'Who knows? My mother did not live long. I remember vaguely that she was no darker than I – although memory, like truth, changes, does it not?'

'I thought you were as good as you had ever been, last night,' he told her.

'I was so nervous I thought I was sick.'

'Did you really believe you were her, then?' he asked. 'Is that how it was?'

She nodded. 'I was not playing, sir. I was everything I wanted to be,' she said. 'I was escaping, I think, being someone strong. She has no worries, Caraboo. I have too many. She was who I would wish to be if dreams were true.'

They had reached the lake. The mare put her head down to drink and Fred patted her neck.

'You are not so angry with me, then?' Mary said.

'I do believe it is hard to keep that fever pitch of anger inside without grinding your teeth down to stumps.'

'I am sorry—'

'Do stop that!' he said, looking away. 'Caraboo never said sorry, did she?'

'No.'

'I liked that about her. Too many girls I know are always sorry for everything, even when it is not their fault.'

'But, sir, doesn't the Bible say we are to blame? For everything?'

'Of course you are. The South Sea Bubble and the French Revolution. Napoleon Bonaparte and our use-less king. It is your fault, everything.' He looked at her. 'See, you are smiling at me now.'

'I had no wish to hurt—'

'We have said all this.'

The mare whickered and swished her tail.

'I wanted Caraboo to be everything I wasn't.' Mary looked at him. 'Brave, mostly. Not afraid of anything. I wanted her to be a person who didn't look down when someone came into the room, who was haughty and bold and true.'

'True? Hah!'

'Perhaps that is the wrong word. But she was true for me, sir.' She sighed. 'I wanted to be her so much that sometimes I really *was* her.'

'But she didn't exist!'

'She was a dream. A good dream that never meant to hurt anyone.'

'You could have hurt Mama . . .' Fred looked away.

'It is the truth that hurts,' she said. 'That always hurts. Give me pretty lies.'

He smiled. 'You may have something there, whoever you are.'

They said nothing for a long time, simply staring back at the house, which seemed a long way off, a shadow on the horizon.

'You know,' Fred said eventually, 'last night I was thinking many things: that we are all liars, in one way or another; that we would all rather be somebody else.'

Mary looked at him, but he was gazing out across the lake, towards the island, his expression unreadable.

'I thought,' he said, 'that if anyone asked me in a week, or a month, or a year, if I would rather a world in which I had never met the Princess Caraboo . . . I am sure I would say no.'

*

When she woke up, Cassandra felt completely refreshed. She had done the right thing and she would think no more about Will. It was a beautiful morning, Diana would be here before lunch, and outside across the park the swallows were diving and soaring. She would wear the blue cotton with the puffed sleeves, and Edmund would admire her very much. She was imagining a boat – a gondola – on a canal in Venice: she was so close to Edmund she could feel his heart beating; but when she looked up, she saw that it was Will Jenkins. She stared at herself in the mirror and pouted. Then, through her window, she caught sight of her brother leading his mare towards the house. He was walking with a girl she didn't recognize, in a very poor black stuff gown. She turned away – it was probably more help from the village for the party tonight.

'Mrs Worrall, your princess is most uncommonly fascinating in every way!' Lady Gresham said at breakfast.

Mrs Worrall blushed. 'You are too kind.'

Lady Gresham acknowledged the reply with a tight smile. 'I have always cultivated an interest in anthropology, a little like yourself. I hope Captain Palmer is quite well,' she said. 'I would so like to talk to him about marriage customs in the islands. Marriage customs are quite my speciality. I have heard tell of a region high in the mountains of the eastern frontiers of India where a woman may have as many husbands as she pleases! Think of that!'

Mrs Worrall nodded. 'I have heard that too.'

Lady Gresham went on, determined to show off her knowledge, 'And I read of a tribe – Africa, India, I cannot recall – where a widow wears her dead husband's head around her neck.'

'Mother, please.' Edmund put down his fork. 'Some of us are eating.' His kedgeree did not look very appetizing any more.

'I wish I could recall the details,' his mother said. 'Perhaps Captain Palmer may elucidate when he is ready to join us. I did so enjoy the tales of . . . what were they called?'

'Penanggalan, Lady Gresham.' Mrs Worrall turned to Fred. 'Fred, darling. Captain Palmer? Have you seen him this morning?'

Edmund nudged him into attention. 'Fred.'

'What? Captain Palmer? No,' he said.

Edmund leaned close and said low, 'I doubt if the man'll be upright anytime before the afternoon, the amount of liquor he downed last night.'

Fred whispered back, 'If that was a bet, you would lose. The man can drink the West Indies dry, and still caper up and down the stairs as if it were nothing!'

'I think it a shame Papa should have to go to work on a Saturday,' Cassandra said.

'Your father has responsibilities, dear,' Mrs Worrall said. 'Although sometimes I do believe he would rather be married to the bank, for all the attention and fuss. But he agrees that you and I – and Fred, if he wishes – may accompany the Princess to Bath, and Mr Hutchinson, of the Scientific and Literary Society – he is travelling here with the Edgecombes – will host an educational evening in the Pump Rooms.'

Lady Gresham nodded approvingly.

Mrs Worrall finished her tea. 'If you will excuse me, Lady Gresham, there is much to be done. Mr Gutch from the *Bristol Advertiser* will be arriving with Mr Barker, the artist, from town. They are bringing the finished portrait. I cannot wait to see it, and Mr Gutch wishes to write a story about the Princess for his paper.'

'Don't you think, Mama,' Fred said, 'it would be as well to ask the girl what she would like?'

Mrs Worrall waved her hand dismissively. 'She will love Bath! Everyone loves Bath!'

'Oh yes, Mama, Bath,' Cassandra said excitedly. 'There is an excellent dressmaker in Bath, Diana says . . .'

Mrs Worrall shook her head. 'Diana says! Dressmakers! You would do well to think of other things!'

Lady Gresham smiled benignly. 'I was much the same at Cassandra's age, and she does carry the fashion well, your daughter.'

Mrs Worrall smiled; Casandra beamed.

'I am certain Caraboo will want to come to Bath, Fred,' Cassandra said. 'Only dull people do not.'

'Does she not join you for breakfast?' asked Lady Gresham.

'Oh no – she catches most of her own food, and cooks it herself,' Mrs Worrall told her. 'I do not doubt that she is at this moment on the roof or up a tree looking for her quarry!'

Edmund sipped his coffee and whispered to Fred, 'That Caraboo – I should like to see her up a tree! As brown as a bloody monkey, your princess!'

Fred got up. 'If you'll excuse me.' As he pushed his chair back, he heard approaching hoofbeats – a messenger, he thought – but was glad to leave the table in any case.

In the yard he found Vaughan and the stable boy trying to catch Zephyr, wild-eyed and in a lather, as if the horse had run all night.

'Catch him!'

'Yes, sir,' Vaughan said, grabbing hold of the bridle, muttering calming, soothing words and stroking the horse's neck. His soft voice worked its magic on the animal, which was soon drinking the fresh water Stephen had brought.

'There, there,' Vaughan cooed. 'What happened to you, eh?'

The horse snorted and shook himself, relaxing under Vaughan's touch.

'What in heaven's name *did* happen, Vaughan?' Fred asked.

'Sorry, sir, we don't know.' He looked at Stephen, who shrugged. 'I thought Miss Cassandra had taken him out for a ride before breakfast, like she used to.'

'Is he all right?'

Vaughan ran his hands down Zephyr's legs and across his back. 'Right as rain, sir, once he's quietened down – just needs some kind words and a soft bed, much like ourselves.'

Fred looked up. Caraboo, or Mary, was watching from the roof. For a moment he caught her eye, then she stepped back, and was gone. Vanished.

The Edgecombes arrived at exactly eleven, by which time Princess Caraboo was in her hunting outfit on the roof, bow and arrow aimed at a particularly plump wood pigeon; Cassandra and Edmund were watching her from the trapdoor. Cassandra waved to her friend and the pigeon took flight. Caraboo was relieved – now that she was so plainly only pretending to be the Princess, her skill with bow and arrow seemed to have diminished.

'Oh, Princess, I am sorry, was that your breakfast?' Cassandra turned and headed for the stairs. 'Diana is here and I must greet her!'

Caraboo saluted. She had hoped Edmund would follow Cassandra, but he leaned casually against the tiles. She ignored him, and busied herself arranging the handful of rose bay willow herb she had picked upon her makeshift altar.

'Cassandra says you speak no English,' he said. She didn't turn round. 'Princess! Princess Caraboo!'

She knew she should look him in the eye as an equal, just as the Princess would have done. But it was hard. How long before Cassandra came back . . . ?

'Oi! Princess, I am talking to you!'

'Caraboo pray,' she said solemnly, turning her back on him. She began her outlandish prayer ceremony, but it felt horribly contrived. She tried to think of Caraboo's god, Allah Tallah, but he was only pretend too; if she turned round, Edmund Gresham would surely read the truth on her face.

'What are you doing up here?' Fred's voice.

Thank God, she thought – she was no longer alone with Edmund. She carried on praying, feeling the knot of muscles in her stomach relax.

'Watching,' Edmund said. 'Although it is a poor show. Mama would love it, but she cannot make the stairs, so I promised I would report back. Perhaps I should make it a little more interesting when I tell her – adding some animal sacrifice, with the reading of entrails.'

Fred laughed, and she could hear that he was relieved too.

After a while Edmund went on, 'Remember that boy at school, the sultan's son, who worshipped a blue elephant?'

Fred nodded, and felt a little ashamed. 'We made that poor boy's life a misery.'

'He deserved it!'

'Did he?'

'Have you forgotten how he got his manservant to threaten me with expulsion?'

Fred shook his head. 'Come down – there is coffee, and Diana Edgecombe's dress is truly a thing of wonder.'

'It's not that confection she wore at the New Year, is it? It was the colour of pea soup, I recall, and after a dance or two with you she coloured up so that she resembled nothing more than salmon mousse upon a bed of lettuce!'

Their voices tailed away and Caraboo was alone again. She got up and brushed the dust off her hunting dress. One more day, that's all – but the days were getting longer and longer . . .

One more evening performance, one more session with Professor Heyford talking about of skulls, believing he could divine character from the shape of a head. She smiled as she thought of it. But perhaps, she told herself, it was no more outrageous than people in the South Seas believing in bloodsucking spirits, or a girl from Devon believing she was a princess.

She could hear noisy preparations for the party going on below her, and resolved that Princess Caraboo would spend the best part of the day upon the island. She would push the rowing boat away from the shore – that way, no one would follow her.

Tucking the kriss into her belt, she made her way down the stairs, carefully, quietly . . . If she was lucky, she could make her way through the house by the back stairs, unseen.

But she was not the only one trying to sneak down the servants' staircase: suddenly she heard footsteps below her. Very carefully, she peered over the banister – and drew back the moment she saw who it was: Captain Palmer.

He had been on his way downstairs, but if he saw

her . . . The last thing she wanted, the last thing she needed, was to be cornered alone on a staircase by that foul man . . .

She forced herself to calm down, and hazarded another glance. The captain had not noticed her, and was creeping slowly and carefully downstairs. He looked as if he were up to something.

She was not really Princess Caraboo, she thought, yet she had been able to move about so quietly that wild animals hadn't heard her until it was too late . . . Even if she was no longer a princess, she could still make sure she was not seen.

Barefoot, silently, and listening carefully to Captain Palmer's footsteps, she started to follow him.

It would be best, Captain Palmer had decided, to cut his losses and take what he could while he still had the chance. The girl was too much of a liability, if what had happened in Bristol was anything to go by. He could threaten her into coming with him, but it was clear that if he let his guard down for even a second, she'd escape his clutches. No, he'd slip what he could into his bags now and dispose of her as soon as he could; make it look as if she'd made off with the valuables, fooling him along with the rest of them. Maybe he'd stay around for a little more free rum and chit-chat, and then be on his merry way unscathed while the constables scoured the docks for a girl they'd never find.

Mrs Worrall's dressing room would be empty now – bound to be rich pickings there; a few of those necklaces would fetch a pretty penny, and their absence would most likely go unnoticed until he'd had the time to get rid of the phoney princess, leave her body in a ditch somewhere no one would find it – or, better, a river . . . And if anybody did find her, they'd assume the pretty little fool had simply been robbed. Cheerful old Captain Palmer would be in the clear.

He cast a quick glance up and down the empty corridor, and then allowed himself a little smile as he pushed open the door. The dressing room couldn't compare with the fashionable Chinoiserie of the drawing room downstairs, but the cabinets, he knew, would yield treasures.

He didn't notice Princess Caraboo standing at the door behind him as he started to ease open one of the drawers.

Caraboo's heart was pounding in her chest as she watched him fill up his bag with Mrs Worrall's jewellery. She'd half expected him to notice her by now, but she was a hunter, a good one, and that was the truth.

It was then that Captain Palmer turned round.

She froze in place, and he smiled. 'Hello, Princess. Looking to claim your part in the loot, eh? Well, too bad. I've decided I don't need you after all, you see. This' – he patted the trinket-stuffed bag at his waist – 'will do me more good than a lying little bitch like you.'

She drew herself up to her full height. She might not have been a real princess but, she realized as she stared at him with his bag of stolen treasure, she was better than he was. Captain Palmer was nothing but a pirate, and if he was so intent on acting the villain, then she could be the brave and cunning Princess one last time. 'I am not a liar,' she hissed. 'Not like you. And I won't let you steal from Mrs Worrall! She is a good woman – these are good people. They have been nothing but courteous to you!'

'Is that so?' the captain sneered, taking a step towards her.

But Caraboo did not want to hear another word of what he had to say. Quick as a cat, she drew her knife to slash at him. He swung out of the way and brought down his fist to knock it out of her hand – but she had not been aiming for his body, and he was too late. The worn leather straps of his bag had been severed by the sharp blade, and as the knife clattered to the floor, Palmer's bag fell too, necklaces and rings spilling out like blood.

His eyes narrowed. 'I'll make you regret that, girl,' he growled, and snatched up her knife.

He was going to kill her, Caraboo thought. Hadn't he just said he had no more use for her? He would kill her. She would not be able to stop him. If she ran for help, he'd pin the blame on her, say he caught *her* in the act; she wouldn't be able to explain without giving herself away.

She needed a weapon.

She thought of her bow and arrow, still on the roof, and began to run.

'So you see, Lady Gresham, phrenology is most definitely the science of the future.' Professor Heyford beamed.

Her ladyship looked bored. 'I have heard some say the same about electricity.'

'Indeed, but in the fullness of time I doubt whether it has the possibilities that phrenology—'

'But electricity has shown to be most beneficial for women with all forms of hysteria,' she said.

'For women, yes, it's true' – he nodded – 'electricity is most therapeutic. The energy given off can impart a most enlivening "kick"!'

Fred looked at the professor and thought that he was as big a liar as Caraboo.

'Professor, your equipment was not a roaring success.' Fred turned to Lady Gresham. 'The Princess was nearly fried to a crisp.'

'No, no, no.' The professor shook his head. 'I think it was merely that the machinery is calibrated for our European heads and brains. Did you not notice, your ladyship, the distinct slope of the Princess's skull, so obviously foreign?'

Fred didn't want to stay and listen to this nonsense any longer. He left the room and went out into the sunshine. It was a perfect summer's day: swallows crisscrossed the high blue sky, and the distant hills shimmered. On the terrace his sister and Diana were giggling over some joke of Edmund's. Fred could hear the wheels and hoof beats of a two-seater coming down the drive. Probably the newspaperman. He should feel content and happy – he was heir to Knole and the Tolzey Bank: a long life of pretence stretched out ahead of him. Pretence that he was happy and that he was a gentleman – when any who looked inside, who saw his heart, would know just how sullied it really was. *Every one of us*, Fred thought, looking at Edmund, *is a liar.*

Suddenly there was a sound, a shout, a girl's voice. He looked up to the roof. He couldn't see a thing except blue sky and swallows and a rain of flowers. He frowned. It was pink willow herb falling from the sky – and something else; something that looked like a solid streak of black ink.

An arrow.

Fred dashed back inside and up the stairs, taking them two, three at a time.

Palmer shut the trapdoor behind him as he stepped out onto the roof after Caraboo. 'Don't want anyone hearing, do we?' he said as, stony faced and more serious than she'd ever seen him, he came towards her. 'Too bad you dropped your knife, *Princess*. You will go down, and I'll tell everyone what a clever liar you were to fool even old Captain Palmer, when all you ever really wanted was the family jewels.'

Caraboo still did not know what she meant to do. But they were on her territory now, and though she was cornered, she felt safer here. More in control.

She snatched up her bow and arrow from where they lay by the altar – but the arrow jumped out of her hand and fell off the roof, tumbling down with the flowers she'd arranged so carefully earlier. Caraboo backed up, breathing hard, but she was too near the edge – there wasn't room, he was cornering her . . . She had been too hasty, and now the chance was gone.

Captain Palmer laughed. 'You owe me,' he said, and there was something dark in his voice. 'I didn't have to play along with your silly games. I could have revealed to everyone what you were, had you thrown out in the street . . .'

Caraboo didn't want to listen. She tried to ram the end of the bow against his neck and get past him, but as she tried to push by, he grabbed her by the elbow with one hand; with the other he disarmed her. He had obviously done this many times before.

'Easy, now . . .' His face was next to hers. She turned away, but he had pressed her up against the tiles.

That was when she screamed. He smothered her cry, his hand over her mouth – *in* her mouth . . . She gagged at the taste of tobacco and spirits – and suddenly the months rolled back and she was face down in the cherry blossom again.

She would not let it happen twice. She bit hard and he cried out, hopping backwards, shaking his hand. 'You little bitch – you drew blood!'

She backed up to the parapet. 'I'll scream again,' she said breathlessly, and he lunged for her, slapping her face so hard it burned. She pushed him away as hard as she could, but then she felt his hands on her body, pulling at her; she pushed again – and it was over.

Fred saw it happen. If he'd got the trapdoor open with the first kick, he thought, he might have been in time. As it was, the captain stumbled, and one foot caught against the altar. He went over the edge and fell, screaming shrilly – reminding Fred of the sound one of their horses had made when it broke its leg.

Then there was a soft, crumpled thud, and the horse pulling the gig that had just drawn up in front of the house whinnied and danced on the gravel.

Captain Palmer was dead.

Caraboo – or Mary, or whoever she was – stood stock still at the edge of the roof, wide eyed and trembling. 'It was an accident, sir,' she said softly, terrified. 'I was trying to stop him – he was going to . . . Please. It was an accident.'

She gathered up the skirts of her plain black dress as she made her way down the drive, away from Knole Park. It was early morning, and there was dew on the ground; the house was asleep, the only noises distant birdsong and the sound of her own footsteps and Fred Worrall's on the gravel.

She'd told Fred he didn't need to walk her down to the road, that he should be back in his bed before anybody else woke, but he had insisted. He'd also insisted on giving her one of Cassandra's old coats, and – he'd smiled when he'd handed it to her – a knife. It wasn't Mrs Worrall's kriss, but a good sharp knife from the kitchen – which, seeing as she was no longer Princess

Caraboo, was far more appropriate. She had tried to turn him down – she'd told him she wanted to leave with nothing more than what she'd arrived with. However, with a wry smile he'd told her that Caraboo had brought such liveliness to their house that it would be impolite to send her on her way with nothing at all.

'It won't even seem strange for her to leave now,' he'd pointed out. 'The Princess was obviously so badly shaken by Captain Palmer's terrible fall that she fled . . .'

'When did you come to know Caraboo better than I do?' Mary had asked, smiling sadly at him, and Fred had laughed, and held out the coat for her again, and the knife, and she had taken them.

Now the coat was warm about her shoulders, the knife tucked safely away underneath. As they came to the road, she started to slow down, and so did Fred. For a long moment they stood together in silence.

'You don't have to go, you know,' he said suddenly. 'You could stay. Go back to being Caraboo. Now that Palmer is gone, no one could stop you.'

She gazed up at him. He was ivory and gold in the morning light, his eyes filled with a longing that said he knew what he was asking was impossible.

She shook her head. 'Caraboo is finished, you know that. I won't lie any more.'

'You wouldn't be lying to me. I'd know.' There was

something desperate in his voice that made her think of Will Jenkins, pleading with Cassandra by the lake. 'You could pretend to learn English; we could—'

'You know I can't. I need to live my own life, not someone else's.'

Fred nodded, a small, sad smile tugging at his lips, and she knew he understood.

'I don't think Caraboo was someone else,' he said, 'not completely.' He touched her face lightly, and with one finger gently lifted her chin so that she was looking him in the eye. 'I think Mary Willcox is every bit as clever and fierce.' And before she could tell him otherwise he was kissing her, softly and wistfully. Her hands found his, and held them tight, twining their fingers together. As their warm breath mingled in the chill air, she knew that for all his sadness, and hers, Fred Worrall's heart would not be broken as Will Jenkins' had been; he would never see her again, but he would always know that she had loved him back.

The sun was beginning to dry the dew off the road. It was a long way yet to Bristol; she'd had an early start but, on foot, it would still be evening before she reached the docks. If she closed her eyes she could see the masts, towering black silhouettes against the shimmering red sky, and beyond them the sea, the horizon. And beyond even that, America . . . She had no idea what that would look like, but she pictured tall buildings in gleaming new cities, where a hard-working, honest girl could make a life for herself no matter where she came from.

Somewhere behind her, Knole Park was waking up, and the end of Princess Caraboo's story was being spun out from what she'd left behind, by those who had wanted to believe in her so much that, for a while, she had been real. And Mary Willcox, of Witheridge, in Devon, near Exeter, carried on westward, with the sunshine warm on her back and the whole world ahead of her.

EPILOGUE

Degroot's Drapers, Haberdashery and General Store
23 Cortlandt Street
New York City
April 1820

'And then,' she said, pausing as she folded the velvet ribbons into place, 'the Princess let fly her arrow straight into the pirate chief's heart!'

'Did he die, Mary? Did he die?' Little Jacob Degroot jumped up and down, tugging at her apron.

Mary finished with the ribbons and began to dust down the dark mahogany counter of the draper's shop.

'No, silly' – his older sister, Martha, made a face – 'that would never have happened.' She pulled her cotton bonnet into place and tied it under her chin. 'Even I know that could never happen and I am seven years old!'

Mary and Jacob exchanged looks.

'Why not? Why not, Martha?' Jacob looked at Mary. 'Martha thinks you made it up – she says you make everything up.'

'They are only Mary's stories, Jacob, and when you start your lessons with Papa, as I have, you will understand that Princess Caraboo is only tales. Tappa Boo and Frederick of the South Seas are all pretend.' Martha turned on her heel, then ran out of the shop and up the stairs at the back.

'Well, what does Miss Martha know?' Mary said, bending down to look at Jacob. 'I don't think she would recognize a princess or a pirate even if she tripped over one, do you?'

Jacob shook his head.

The door jingled as it opened, and the post boy from the office round the corner in Liberty Street smiled as he stepped into the shop. 'Delivery, miss!' He left the parcel on the counter top and winked at Jacob, and then at Mary.

After he'd gone, Jacob tugged at her apron. 'Martha says he is sweet on you.'

'He is not!' Mary scolded. 'Martha scorns my tales but loves to spin her own!'

She straightened up. The shop looked perfect. She sighed, a half happy sigh: she loved New York City . . . if only Devon and the ones she loved were not so far away.

But there were worse places. In New York City it was as if all the world had met in one place. It reminded her of London, if London had been put together with considerably more haste. She loved the fashions: whalers in skins in winter, traders from the north in dark sables, women from the East in such wonderful embroidery. Most of them on their way farther west or out to sea.

She'd seen pictures of farther west, the land where everyone went to seek their fortunes. The woman next door's husband was an artist – she had never set eyes on him, for he travelled all over the country, painting the native people, mostly. The house was full of his paintings. They made her think of Mrs Worrall, who would no doubt have redecorated her Chinese drawing room around one of those images. Perhaps when she had made her own fortune, out west somewhere, she would send one to Knole Park as a present, to make up for everything.

The pictures reminded her of Caraboo, and a short life lived half a world away.

She had not swum, or climbed, or eaten roasted pigeon, for close on a year, and the urge to live a wilder life had begun to rise in her.

Mr Degroot was a good man, a widower whose wife was dead, and who could not afford more than one extra pair of hands: Mary worked in the shop, cleaned and cooked, and looked after the children. She worried a little about what might happen if she did leave, but ever since Christmas, when he'd had one glass of advocaat too many and asked her to marry him, Mary thought it would be best to move on. She hadn't saved quite enough money yet, and in any case he had never mentioned it again. But still, she thought, some day soon she would go west, into the sun, with a party of travellers . . .

She sighed and began unwrapping the parcel. It would be trimmings of some kind – that new lace edging Mr Degroot was waiting for. The box was easy enough to open, but inside, the lace – it was handmade and the best quality – had been wrapped in layer upon layer of tissue. And oh! It was beautiful! She held some up to the light and gasped, it was so perfect. She laid it out flat. It was fit for the finest wedding dresses. She could imagine an East Side princess walking down the aisle in a dress dripping with this lace trim.

She was still absorbed in the material when the door tinkled again, and she almost didn't notice the new arrival until the man spoke.

'Mary?' he said.

She knew him at once. Tall and, when he took off his hat, fair – no, golden haired, blue eyed. Someone she thought she'd never see again. She had to lean on the counter to stop her legs giving way.

'Mr Worrall,' she said, trying to compose herself. 'You are here?'

He put a hand out to touch her face, and she stood frozen for a moment before moving away.

'I never did thank you. I wrote so many letters, but could not send them.' Mary looked away. 'Is Mrs Worrall well? And Cassandra? I was thinking about her only this morning . . .'

He smiled. 'All, eventually,' he said. 'You made quite a stir when the papers printed your story, and Mama was inconsolable – until Christmas, when Cassandra announced a rather early wedding to Edmund Gresham.'

'No! I thought he was travelling?'

'His grand tour was somewhat curtailed after he came down with something nasty in Leghorn.'

Mary took a deep breath, and sat down. 'I was worried, you know, about them all,' she said. 'I know it was the wrong—'

'Stop it.'

'But you saved me from jail . . .'

He shook his head. 'The papers were all on your side. They thought Princess Caraboo a phenomenon.' He paused. 'They loved you. You had a score of imitators in every penny gaff in every city.'

At that moment Jacob Degroot came rushing downstairs, in floods of tears. 'Martha says I am stupid!'

Mary scooped him up and dried his tears with the edge of her apron. 'Well, you are not.' She turned him round to face Fred. 'This is my friend, Mr Frederick Worrall.'

'Frederick? Is he a pirate, like in stories?' Jacob said.

Mary blushed. 'Absolutely not!'

'Delighted to meet you.' Fred put out his hand for the boy to shake. 'I've come all the way from England to see Mary.'

'Across the sea? Did you find any pirates?'

'Luckily no, not a one. But it seems I have found Mary, eventually.'

'You shouldn't have,' she said. 'You do not know me – I am nothing.'

'You are not nothing!' Jacob said.

'You are so right, young sir,' Fred said. 'And in any case, I know someone who knew Mary very well, in England. And I never really understood, but that person made me so sad when she left that I could not live without her. I could not study, I could not think, I could not sleep,' he said.

'Who was that?' Jacob said.

'A princess,' said Fred.

'A real one?'

'No, Jacob, he's just playing,' Mary said.

'I'm not. I do assure you, she was a real princess,' Fred said. 'A beautiful, fearless warrior princess.'

'Really?'

'She spoke her own language – one nobody in the whole world had ever heard – and she could climb the tallest trees, and she was a crack shot too. She could bring a pigeon down with a bow and arrow.'

'Like Princess Caraboo! She *was* real! Wait till I tell Martha!' Jacob's eyes were as wide as saucers. 'So, what happened to her?'

'I don't know,' said Fred. His eyes met Mary's and she couldn't look away; he was lovely, a million times better than the memory. 'That's why I'm here in New York – to find her and ask her to make a new life. If we can . . .'

Author's Note

The true story of Princess Caraboo is completely unbelievable and utterly amazing. I have had to tweak and stuff her real life into a novel, but I'd like to add a note to give you a taste of the stuff I've had to leave out.

When the tale emerged in the summer of 1817, Princess Caraboo became a newspaper sensation; after all, who could resist a girl from the street who had managed to hoodwink professors and academics – who had outwitted the upper classes? There were poems and articles, and whole books about her were rushed out to cash in.

But Mary Wilcox was not really a con woman. She never attempted to make any money out of her stay at the Worralls'. In fact, as in the book, she tried to leave Knole Park. And Mrs Worrall obviously cared deeply for her: she paid for Mary's fare to America, and treasured the letters Mary sent back; she was the daughter Elizabeth Worrall never had (in reality she only had sons).

My account doesn't follow Mary's life in every respect. I've changed the date, and Mary's age; Cassandra never existed. But most of the bones of the story are firmly based in truth; even the language Caraboo uses in my book is the one Mary Wilcox made up herself.

The real Mary Wilcox was in her twenties and had suffered a great deal. She'd been married and abandoned; she had given birth alone, handing her baby over to the Foundling Hospital. She underwent an early form of surgery to her head, in the most horrific and brutal of London workhouses, and bore the scars.

She was also, it seems, an inveterate liar and teller of tales. She embroidered the truth when she had to, whether it was to secure a place for her child at the Foundling Hospital or a bed in a home for reformed prostitutes.

I relied on many books in researching her story, but it's clear that the story changed depending on who she was talking to – and when. If you're interested in as much of the truth as possible, the best source has to be *Princess Caraboo – Her True Story* by John Wells.

After her unmasking Mary Wilcox was described as follows:

. . . eyes and hair black; complexion a brunette; her
cheeks faintly tinged with red; mouth rather wide;
lips large and full.

This description is from a book rushed out a few weeks after she was revealed not to be a princess but a cobbler's daughter from Witheridge in Devon. The book, *Caraboo: A Narrative of a Singular Imposition*, was by John Mathew Gutch, a newspaper editor on the *Bristol Journal*. She seems to have been dark skinned, even though one of her portraits shows her as fair.

We know that she was born in a small Devon village, that she could read and write and worked for a while as a children's nanny, first in Exeter and then in London.

One of the families she worked for took her to France for a while; another family in London lived next door to Orthodox Jews, and Mary made friends. She loved the weddings and the ceremony and the chanting. In fact, she got the sack for attending a Jewish wedding.

She was married, then abandoned; but was her husband the father of her child? We can't say. She claimed first that he was a bricklayer; then that he was an educated man she met in a bookshop; then a Frenchman. Everyone Mary Wilcox spoke to was given a slightly different story. In one she was seduced, and delivered her baby on the road. In another she was with the father for nine months.

She had to give up her baby (called John Francis, then rechristened Edward King) to the Foundling Hospital in London (where no doubt she gave a version of her tale that would ensure he was accepted). The child was admitted on 1 July, and Mary went to visit him every week until he died in October.

She also spent time in the Magdalen Hospital in South London, a kind of refuge for girls who had been working as prostitutes. They wore old-fashioned clothes: broad-brimmed straw hats, white caps and long brown dresses. In order to be admitted, girls had to confess to their life of sin. However, it's unclear whether Mary worked on the streets – though it is not completely unlikely. John Wells says of her application to enter the Magdalen Hospital that 'she had imagined the plot of an entire novel of betrayed love. As usual it probably contained strands of truth.' She herself said she'd applied to live there simply because she loved the clothes.

Mary loved dressing up. She came across Normandy lace-makers who wore intricate headdresses, and decided, for the purposes of begging, to pretend to be French. She told one interviewer that she had even travelled to Bombay.

When Mary was found in Almondsbury, wearing her

turban, uttering not a word. As in my story, Mrs Worrall was American, and intelligent. Married to a banker and probably bored out of her mind, she must have looked on Caraboo as the most interesting person she had ever met.

But in reality, at first Mrs Worrall couldn't persuade her husband to let Caraboo stay; she was sent to the Bristol workhouse. Caraboo suffered dreadfully there – and still didn't speak a word of English – and when Mrs Worrall heard, she begged her husband to bring the girl home. A Portuguese traveller passing through Bristol visited Knole Park and declared that she was from the East Indies; he had spoken to her in her own language – the girl was a princess who had been kidnapped by pirates and swam ashore, he said.

The Worralls were convinced; I think they must have *wanted* to be convinced – her tale must have seemed so exciting. Dr Charles Wilkinson, a specialist in 'Electrical Medicine', was one of the many academics and interested intellectuals who appeared at Knole to see the Princess. Mrs Worrall had the daughter she wanted, and such a fascinating one . . .

The Worralls' second son, Fred, home from Westminster School and on his way to a career in the Army, thought her a fraud, but the rest of the household was soon won over. The Worralls gave Caraboo the run of the house and she was very entertaining. She was pretty, she danced, she made exotic outfits for herself; she swam, she climbed trees and was expert with a bow and arrow.

Mrs Worrall had a library of books about exciting noble savages from all over world, including the wonderful *Pantagraphia* – a study of every language, along with examples of its script.

For a clever young woman like Caraboo, it was easy to please her hosts.

It was Charles Wilkinson who proved to be her undoing. He saw the opportunity of lecture tours, of fame and fortune, and encouraged the newspapers to report Caraboo's story. And it was on the eve of his first public lecture in Bath that the truth was revealed: one of Mary's old landladies recognized her description. The game was up.

With the backing of Mrs Worrall, Mary fled to America. A tour of city theatres was arranged for her, giving talks about her time as Caraboo, but she was not a success. Perhaps America was already too full of Europeans inventing new and exciting personas for themselves.

But the British newspapers couldn't get enough of Caraboo. One story even claimed that the ship taking Mary to America had stopped off at St Helena, the remote island where Napoleon had been exiled by the British. According to the newspapers, Caraboo had bewitched him; they even hinted at a possible romance.

The reality is that she lived in Philadelphia and began using her married name, Mary Baker. We don't know exactly how long she stayed in the States – possibly until 1824 or 1825 – but there is evidence that at some point she reappeared in New Bond Street, London, as Princess Caraboo. After this report Mary Wilcox/Baker fades out of public life completely.

But thanks to John Wells's research we know how Mary ended her life. She remarried another man called Baker – and Wells likes to imagine that this is the same man she first married all those years ago, pre Caraboo. At her death on 31 December 1864 she was a widow, with a grown-up daughter and a flourishing business selling medicinal leeches to the Bristol Infirmary.

Her story is astounding for so many reasons: here is a girl who won't be bound by the constraints of her birth; who re-invents herself; who dreams herself into a new existence and makes the world believe her, even if only for a little while.

ABOUT THE AUTHOR

Catherine Johnson is a born-and-bred Londoner who no longer lives in London but by the sea. She studied film at Central Saint Martins School of Art; the fantastic time she had there made up for school, which was horrible.

She has written many books for young readers, and her recent novel, *Sawbones*, published by Walker Books, won the Young Quills Award for historical fiction and was nominated for the Carnegie Medal. Her other books include *Brave New Girl* (Frances Lincoln Children's Books), and *A Nest of Vipers*, published by Random House Children's Publishers UK.

Catherine has also written for film, notably the critically acclaimed *Bullet Boy*, and TV, including *Holby City*.

She lives with her husband and two geriatric pets: a deluded cat and an ancient tortoise. She enjoys baking cakes and knitting. She was taught how to drive (horses, not cars) by an ex-brewery dray driver in Spitalfields.

Also available from
Random House Children's Publishers UK
A Nest of Vipers

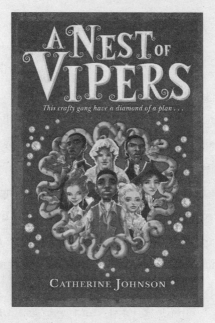

Cato Hopkins is the youngest member of Mother Hopkins's
'family' – a group of skilled fraudsters and pickpockets.
There's Addy, who can become a very convincing boy when
she needs to; the beautiful Bella, who can charm any rich
young man out of his fortune; Sam, an escaped slave
and Cato himself, a young boy, who Mother Hopkins
has taught everything she knows.

But old age is slowing Mother Hopkins down, and she
wants to carry out one last con, a con to outdo all the
cons that have gone before. And so the gang set about
bringing ruin upon Captain Walker, a proud and cruel
slave captain, who deserves to be taught a lesson or two . . .

'A characterful, page-turning drama and a vivid mixture
of research and imagination' – *The Sunday Times*

Read Catherine's story 'The Liar's Girl' in
Love Hurts
edited by Malorie Blackman

Malorie Blackman brings together the best teen
writers of today in a stunningly romantic collection
about love against the odds. Featuring short stories and
extracts – both brand-new and old favourites – about
star-crossed lovers from stars such as Gayle Forman,
Markus Zusak, Patrick Ness, Catherine Johnson and
Andrew Smith, and with a new story from Malorie Blackman
herself, *Love Hurts* looks at every kind of relationship,
from first kiss to final heartbreak.

'A gorgeously romantic treat' – *The Bookseller*

Also available
Noughts & Crosses
by Malorie Blackman

Sephy is a Cross – a member of the dark-skinned
ruling class. Callum is a nought – a 'colourless' member
of the underclass who were once slaves to the Crosses.

The two have been friends since early childhood.
But that's as far as it can go. Against a background
of prejudice, distrust and mounting terrorist violence, a
romance builds between Sephy and Callum – a romance
that is to lead both of them into terrible danger . . .

'Dramatic, moving and brave' – *Guardian*

Also available
The Accident Season
by Moira Fowley-Doyle

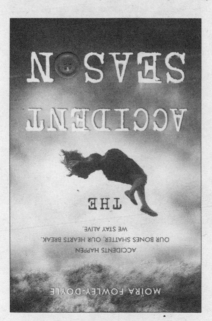

It's the accident season, the same time every year.
Bones break, skin tears, bruises bloom.

The accident season has been part of seventeen-year-old Cara's life for as long as she can remember. Towards the end of October, foreshadowed by the deaths of many relatives before them, Cara's family becomes inexplicably accident-prone. They banish knives to locked drawers, cover sharp table edges with padding, switch off electrical items – but injuries follow wherever they go, and the accident season becomes an ever-growing obsession and fear.

Why are they so cursed?

And how can they break free?

Also available
The Last Leaves Falling
by Sarah Benwell

And these are they. My final moments.
They say a warrior must always be mindful of death,
but I never imagined that it would find me like this . . .

Japanese teenager Sora is diagnosed with ALS (Lou Gehrig's disease). Lonely and isolated, Sora turns to the ancient wisdom of the samurai for guidance and comfort. But he also finds hope in the present; through the internet he finds friends that see him, not just his illness. This is a story of friendship and acceptance, and testing strength in an uncertain future.

'Beautifully written, heartbreaking and hopeful' – *The Bookseller*